Gail looked around, trying to focus, but actually not seeing anything but the hill and some trees and the blue of the ocean beyond.

"I must have bumped my head," Gail said. "I'm having trouble focusing."

"That will pass," Jewel said.

"How do you know?" Gail asked staring into the woman's green eyes. "Are you a doctor?"

"Actually, she is," the guy in purple said. "But that's not why it will pass."

"Then why?" Gail asked, slowly starting to get angry.

"Because you're dead, that's why," a voice said from behind her.

She turned to look into the dark brown eyes of the most handsome man she had ever seen. He looked like he had come right out of court and had just taken off his tie. He had perfectly styled brown hair and those large brown eyes were places to get lost in. His dark suit was made of silk, as clearly was his shirt, and he had on expensive shoes Gail was convinced were not sold anywhere in Oregon.

"I'm Dan, but a lot of my friends just call me Sunset."

The Ghost of a Chance Series

(READING ORDER)

Though these books can be read in any order as they are all stand alone stories, this is the order in which they were written:

The Poker Chip: A Ghost of a Chance Novel

The Christmas Gift: A Ghost of a Chance Novel

The Free Meal: A Ghost of a Chance Novel

The Cop Car: A Ghost of a Chance Novella

The Deep Sunset: A Ghost of a Chance Novel

Also by Dean Wesley Smith

THE POKER BOY UNIVERSE

GHOST OF A CHANCE

The Poker Chip: A Ghost of a Chance Novel

The Christmas Gift: A Ghost of a Chance Novel

The Free Meal: A Ghost of a Chance Novel

The Cop Car: A Ghost of a Chance Novella

The Deep Sunset: A Ghost of a Chance Novel

POKER BOY

The Slots of Saturn: A Poker Boy Novel

They're Back: A Poker Boy Short Novel

Luck Be Ladies: A Poker Boy Collection

Playing a Hunch: A Poker Boy Collection

A Poker Boy Christmas: A Poker Boy Collection

MARBLE GRANT

The First Year: A Marble Grant Novel

Time for Cool Madness: Six Crazy Marble Grant Stories

PAKHET JONES

The Big Tom: A Packet Jones Short Novel

Big Eyes: A Packet Jones Short Novel

THUNDER MOUNTAIN

Thunder Mountain

Monumental Summit

Avalanche Creek

The Edwards Mansion

Lake Roosevelt

Warm Springs

Melody Ridge

Grapevine Springs

The Idanha Hotel

The Taft Ranch

Tombstone Canyon

Dry Creek Crossing

Hot Springs Meadow

Green Valley

SEEDERS UNIVERSE

Dust and Kisses: A Seeders Universe Prequel Novel

Against Time

Sector Justice

Morning Song

The High Edge

Star Mist

Star Rain

Star Fall

Starburst

Rescue Two

COLD POKER GANG

Kill Game

Cold Call

Calling Dead

Bad Beat

Dead Hand

Freezeout

Ace High

Burn Card

Heads Up

Ring Game

Bottom Pair

The Deep Sunset: A Ghost of a Chance Novel

Copyright © 2017 by Dean Wesley Smith

First published in a different form in Smith's Monthly #10, *July, 2014*

Published by WMG Publishing

Cover and Layout copyright © 2024 by WMG Publishing

Cover design by Stephanie Writt | WMG Publishing

Cover Art Designed by Lost Souls Studio

ISBN-13 (trade paperback): 978-1-56146-989-5
ISBN-13 (hardcover): 978-1-56146-990-1

The Deep Sunset

A GHOST OF A CHANCE NOVEL

DEAN WESLEY SMITH

wmg
PUBLISHING

For Kris.
Even more popcorn for the brain

The Deep Sunset

PART ONE

A Meet Cute But Dead

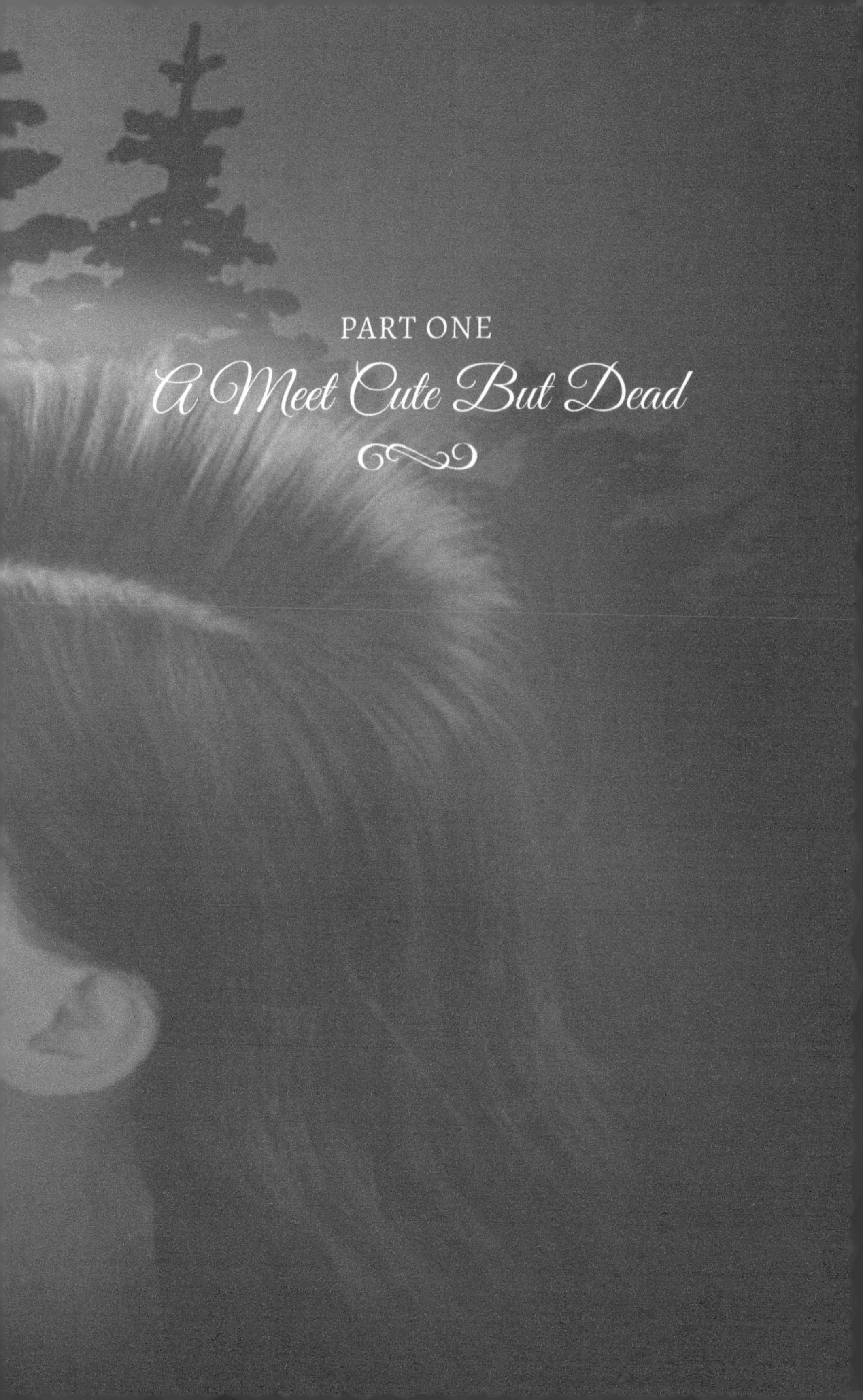

One

You never plan on dying.

Well, at least when you are young you never plan on it.

Gail Kelly sure hadn't. She was twenty-eight, still slim and single, and still very happy in her job as a prosecuting attorney in a small Oregon coastal county. And she was really good at it as well.

Dying was a long ways from her thinking. In fact, marriage and kids were still a long ways from her thinking. She didn't even have a steady boyfriend.

So when that chip truck came across the center line on a curve on Highway 101 and hit her before she could even blink, she didn't have time to think about dying then either.

It just happened so fast.

One minute she was driving her wonderful red BMW convertible, headed south to meet some friends for some drinks and dinner, the next she was sitting on the soft hillside next to the highway.

A very friendly woman about Gail's age was kneeling next to her, smiling. And a handsome man stood on the highway, watching. Standing beside him was a short guy dressed in a purple jogging suit who looked completely out of place on the rough Oregon coast.

Both the man and the woman looked comfortable, dressed in jeans and expensive shirts and running shoes.

"Go slow," the woman next to her said.

"So what happened?" Gail asked, trying to look around, but only seeing the three people and the edge of the highway. The pine forest around her and the ocean below seemed to be a blur.

"You were in an accident," the woman said.

Gail looked down at herself, her legs, her arms. Nothing seemed to be bleeding.

She had on a blue silk blouse with a jogging bra under it, jeans, and her best Nike running shoes. There didn't seem to be a mark or scratch anywhere. The road was a good ten feet below her. Why she would have climbed up here was beyond her.

And she felt fine.

Gail stood and the woman helped her up with a gentle touch on her arm. The two of them went down the soft hillside and through a slight ditch to where the handsome man and the guy in purple stood on the pavement.

"I'm Jewel," the woman said. "This is my partner, Tommy."

The good-looking man nodded and smiled slightly at Gail. He had short military-cut brown hair and broad shoulders. Gail could see in his eyes that he was worried about her.

"This is K.J.," Jewel said, indicating the short man with the purple jogging suit. Now that Gail was closer, she could also see that the man's hair was purple and his shoes were purple and he wore purple fingernail polish. Wow, she hoped he wasn't going into any bars along this coast. He didn't fit. In fact, she had a hunch this K.J. person didn't fit anywhere outside of San Francisco.

K.J. just nodded and smiled, showing purple caps on his teeth.

Gail looked around, trying to focus, but actually not seeing anything but the hill and some trees and the blue of the ocean beyond.

"I must have bumped my head," Gail said. "I'm having trouble focusing."

"That will pass," Jewel said.

"How do you know?" Gail asked staring into the woman's green eyes. "Are you a doctor?"

"Actually, she is," the guy in purple said. "But that's not why it will pass."

"Then why?" Gail asked, slowly starting to get angry.

"Because you're dead, that's why," a voice said from behind her.

She turned to look into the dark brown eyes of the most handsome man she had ever seen. He looked like he had come right out of court and had just taken off his tie. He had perfectly styled brown hair and those large brown eyes were places to get lost in. His dark suit was made of silk, as clearly was his shirt, and he had on expensive shoes Gail was convinced were not sold anywhere in Oregon.

"I'm Dan, but a lot of my friends just call me Sunset."

Gail was convinced those brown eyes of his were seeing right through her. Because of that, it took her a moment to realize what he had said.

"Dead?"

"Oh, nice timing, Sunset," the guy in purple said, clearly disgusted.

The handsome man nodded to Gail, ignoring the guy in purple. "Afraid so. But trust me, you're going to love it."

Sunset smiled at her as he took her elbow and turned her up the road. Suddenly, everything came into clear focus around her.

The evening still had some light as the sun had just set over the ocean. The forest was on her left, the sea down a steep cliff on her right. She could see what was left of her wonderful convertible under the front of a large truck right in the middle of the two-lane highway.

Someone was hosing the entire thing down with a fire extinguisher and a number of others were standing to one side, most with their hands over their mouths.

She could see part of her body twisted in an unnatural way against the grill of the truck. And the truck driver had come about halfway through the window of his truck and was still just hanging there. He looked dead or almost dead.

The sight was so horrific, it took her a moment to realize that was her against the front of the truck.

Holy shit, Sunset was right.

She was dead.

How could that even be possible?

She turned to face him and her knees started to give out.

Sunset and Jewel caught her and eased her to the ground.

"So, Sunset, what are you doing here?" K.J asked.

Jewel held Gail's arm and Tommy, her partner had stepped back.

"Here to train Gail," Sunset said.

Gail had her head down and was focusing on just breathing. She knew this feeling from having too many drinks and she knew just solid breaths of air would help.

"Jewel and Tommy train the new recruits," K.J. said.

"Not this time," Sunset said.

"Train me to do what?" Gail asked, finally letting the anger come out as she stood. She didn't need any training.

Jewel patted Gail's shoulder and stepped back.

"To be dead and worthwhile," Sunset said, smiling at her.

"How about I be *not* dead?" Gail said.

"Not really possible," Sunset said, pointing in the direction of the wreck. "It was your time. See the truck driver? It's almost his time as well. Watch."

Sunset turned her toward the wreck again as suddenly the truck driver sort of moved away from the cab of his truck while his body still remained sticking out of the window.

For a moment he seemed perfectly healthy even though his body in the window clearly wasn't.

Then the driver looked upward and sort of floated in the air and after a moment was gone.

"So how come I don't float out of here?" Gail asked. "And get away from you nut-jobs."

She was angry and scared, but mostly angry, and when angry, she pulled no punches.

"The powers-that-be think you would be a good help in saving people," Jewel said, her voice gentle.

"I don't save people," Gail said, her voice stern. "I put people in jail."

"Sometimes that's saving people," Sunset said, smiling at her and clearly ignoring her anger. "You hungry?"

That question surprised her. "I thought you said I was dead."

"Oh, you are," Sunset said. "And from here on out, the food tastes better."

"You are just confusing Gail," Jewel said, stepping up and putting herself between Gail and those amazing brown eyes.

"I did just fine when I died," Sunset said.

"That's not what I heard," K.J. said.

Gail glanced over. The little guy in purple clearly had some issues with Sunset.

Sunset was about to say something when Jewel raised her hand. "Not here, not now. You can help in Gail's training, if she wants help, but not until I say so."

Gail was impressed. Jewel clearly was the one in charge here.

Sunset looked at Jewel who clearly wasn't backing down.

Finally he nodded to Jewel and smiled at Gail. "See you soon I hope."

Gail was so confused, all she could do was nod.

Then Sunset just vanished right in front of her eyes.

"I'm having the weirdest damn dream," Gail said, deciding to sit down once again on the pavement.

Jewel helped her down and then looked at K.J. "Find out what that was all about. We'll be at the Golden Nugget having dinner."

K.J. nodded and then the little guy in purple also just vanished.

"I haven't even had a drink yet," Gail said, shaking her head.

Then she looked up at her twisted body against the front of the truck and wondered if she would ever drink again.

Two

Sunset appeared on his favorite stool at the Sushi bar in Fong's Restaurant just off Broadway in Portland. He was angry at himself. He had screwed up something awful with that introduction and he knew better than to go up against Jewel and Tommy and K.J.

Sunset had been a Ghost of a Chance agent as long as K.J. Actually, slightly longer since Sunset died in 1901 and K.J. hadn't shown up until few years later.

But Jewel and Tommy were already forces in the agency, even though they were fairly new. They had worked with Poker Boy and others, which was far more than Sunset had ever done. Up until just a few years ago, he hadn't even known the superhero part of all this existed.

Sunset always liked to work alone and he had done just fine that way for over a hundred years. But now, the powers-that-be had told him he was getting a partner even though he had no desire for one.

He hadn't expected his new partner to be so beautiful. That had caught him by surprise, but was still no excuse for him being a jerk. He had figured she could just stand the blunt truth.

He knew she was smart. He had researched her life a little and knew she was still single, a prosecuting attorney with almost a perfect record, and she liked her drinks.

Sunset liked his drinks as well, which is how he had gotten his name. He loved to drink tequila sunsets, which was basically like a tequila sunrise with tequila and orange juice, only instead of the sweet red grenadine syrup that sunk to the bottom of the orange juice, a red soda water was put on the top, holding the red to the top of glass.

And it was a lot less sweet than a sunrise. He had started drinking them back when he worked the New York area after the Second World War. No bar out west served them regularly, so he made them in his Portland condo for himself. He never seemed to tire of them.

He grabbed a plate of California rolls as a waitress carried it past and started to work on them. He loved how, as a ghost, he could eat the ghost part of any meal and no one knew he was doing it.

And the ghost part of a meal tasted so much better than a regular meal ever had when he was alive.

He sat eating and thinking about Gail and how they were going to have to work together and how, now after seeing her, he actually wanted to try to work with her.

Damn, he wished he hadn't screwed up the introduction.

He needed to do something about his mistake and do it now.

He pushed what was left of the sushi roll aside and stood.

"Come on, Sunset. You can do humility. Honestly you can."

With that he jumped to the Golden Nugget Buffet in Las Vegas. He was going to apologize and see if he could help in her training, see if he and Gail really could be a team.

He didn't do apologies that often. As a Ghost Agent, working alone, he had never really needed to. But he had a hunch with Gail, it would be worth taking his pride down a few notches.

Three

One minute Gail had been on the main coastal highway in Oregon looking at an ugly wreck that she had supposedly been in, then she found herself standing near a wooden table in a well-lit buffet.

The smell of fresh beef and baking bread surrounded her and a low level of talking filled the air.

The buffet was all in brown wood tones and bright polished brass. It was a huge place and the table they were beside was in one corner and a distance away from any other people.

The place was comfortable, even though impossible. Gail knew for a fact she couldn't be here.

Yet it seemed she was.

It sure felt and smelled and sounded like she was.

Jewel and Tommy were both standing beside her.

"How did we get here and where is here?" Gail asked after looking around.

"The Golden Nugget Buffet in downtown Las Vegas," Jewel said, indicating that Gail should take a seat. Jewel pulled the chair out slightly for her. "We jumped you here from Oregon."

"I'll get us some water," Tommy said and turned away.

Gail sat down facing the buffet area and Jewel sat beside her at the four-person square table.

"This is the strangest dream I have ever had," Gail said, shaking her head.

None of this was making any sense to her. Not a bit of it. She hadn't even had dinner yet, so it couldn't be something she ate. And she really didn't know anyone or had even been to Las Vegas before, so a place her dream would take her shouldn't be here.

"We all think this is a dream at first," Jewel said. "I know I did."

"So did I," Tommy said, handing Gail a glass of water and then giving Jewel one as well.

Gail made herself take a long drink. The water tasted pure and fresh and wonderful. Best glass of plain water she had ever had.

Now she knew she was dreaming when water tasted good.

Jewel must have been reading her expression. "You think that was good, wait until you taste the food."

"So the Sunset guy was right?" Gail asked.

"He was," Jewel said.

Right at that moment Gail noticed that Jewel had a classically beautiful face and eyes that seemed to really show kindness. And clearly she and Tommy, who also had a classic handsomeness about him, were a team.

"Who is he?" Gail asked as Sunset's handsome face and perfectly dressed body came clearly back to her mind.

"He's another Ghost Agent like we are," Jewel said. "Like you'll be if you decide to stay after you learn everything."

Gail just shook her head. "You know how silly that sounds?"

Jewel nodded and smiled. "Very silly. But very serious at the same time."

"Okay," Gail said, ignoring that her stomach was rumbling just twenty minutes after she had supposedly died, "until I wake up, I'll play along. What do Ghost Agents do?"

"We save people," Jewel said.

Beside her Tommy just nodded.

"Yet we are ghosts?" Gail asked.

Jewel and Tommy both nodded.

Gail shook her head. All this silliness was impossible to believe. She must have caught a horrid bug and was feverish and in a hospital somewhere. Fever dreams were the only thing that could make any of this make sense.

And if she was having a bad fever dream she would think of dying. That made sense.

"Let me see if I can show you a few things," Tommy said.

He stood, then walked right through the table in front of Gail as if it wasn't there.

Then he walked over to a couple starting to leave and let them walk through him.

Then he came back and sat down. He was frowning and Jewel noticed it as well.

Jewel reached over and put her hand on Tommy's arm.

"That older couple that went through me just had their last meal," Tommy said. "They have used the last of their money. They have a gun in their car."

Gail felt stunned. "How do you know that?"

"When you touch a living person, you can read their thoughts," Jewel said, not looking away from Tommy.

"I'm going to follow them," Tommy said, standing. "See if I can figure out something to do."

"What can he do?" Gail asked.

"So many things," Jewel said. "And so few at the same time."

At that moment Sunset arrived, standing to one side of the table. His silk suit was perfect, his shirt open under the suit jacket, and he had a slight look of worry in his large brown eyes.

Gail felt a jolt go through her as she looked up at him. She had never had that reaction to a man before, ever. More than likely part of her fever dream.

And he looked slightly startled as well, then nodded to her and turned to Jewel. "If I apologize for my boorish behavior on the coast, and promise to behave myself and help where I can, may I join you?"

Jewel nodded and smiled, indicating he should take a seat next to Gail.

Then Jewel stood. "Tommy's going to need my help with that couple. I'll be back when I can."

And she vanished.

"What couple?" Sunset asked.

"An elderly couple that walked through Tommy when he was trying to convince me I'm not dreaming," Gail said. "Tommy said the couple had just had their last meal and were out of money and he wasn't sure what they were going to do next."

"Oh, no," Sunset said softly.

"Is that what you ghosts do? Save old folks from themselves?"

Sunset nodded, clearly serious. "Sometimes that, sometimes more. Jewel and Tommy and K.J., along with a superhero and his team and a few of the gods helped save the world just three months ago."

"Saved the world?" Gail asked, ignoring the gods and the superhero part.

Sunset nodded and looked at her for the first time since she sat down. "Jewel will tell you all about it at some point. But I want to apologize for my first meeting. I hope you will give me a second chance to get off on the right foot."

Gail smiled and offered her hand.

"I'm Gail," she said.

He took her hand and instantly she felt a surge of pleasurable electrical force going through her.

"I'm Sunset," he said, clearly noticing the connection.

They sat there for a moment like that, holding the handshake, then he pulled his hand away and looked down.

She felt instant disappointment.

They sat in silence for a long moment, then she finally said, "How do I wake up from this?"

He looked at her, was about to say something, then clearly changed his mind.

"We need food," he said, offering his hand to her as he stood. "Let me show you how ghosts get our food."

"Ghosts are hungry?" she asked, glad he was again holding her hand. If this was a dream, she might as well enjoy it.

"We get hungry, we sleep, and we have to use the bathroom," he said. "Nothing changes on any of that except that no one can see us except other Ghost Agents."

"And we can read people's thoughts?" she asked.

"That," he said, leading her toward the buffet, "and so much more. You'll see. Jewel will train you."

"You're not going to help?" she asked.

"I'll help as much as you would like me to," he said.

"I would like you to," she said.

He nodded and smiled.

"I'll do my best."

And with that, once again they returned to silence. But he was still holding her hand as they made their way around all the tables toward the buffet.

And that felt right.

Oh, oh so right.

Four

Sunset was excited that maybe he had made up for some of his behavior out on the highway. And he was stunned at the connection he and Gail had. Her touch had sent shivers through him like no other ever had in a hundred years.

That was exciting all by itself. He couldn't believe how attracted he was to her.

As they got near the buffet, he said to her, "Be careful not to touch anyone else."

"Read their thoughts?" she asked.

"Just give it some time before you do that. Let Jewel be here to help you through some of those issues."

"Have you ever trained anyone?" she asked. Then she laughed. "I'm acting as if this dream is all real."

"Pretending for the moment it is real," Sunset said, "the answer is no."

They stopped in front of the plates. There was one plate sitting to one side of a stack of others.

"Pick that one up," he said, pointing to the single plate.

She did, holding a plate in her hand.

He pointed at the plate also still sitting there.

"How?" Gail said, looking at the plate in her hand and then the one on the counter.

"You are holding the ghost version of that plate," Sunset said. "Everything has a ghost version."

She stared at the plate in her hand. "It feels real."

"It is, except no one can see it. And if you put it down, after a half day or so it will vanish."

She just nodded and he moved them along to where there were some pizza slices that looked pretty good. He took one slice and she just stared at where the slice still remained on the serving tray.

And yet there was the same exact slice on his plate.

It was at that moment, when neither of them had been paying any attention, that a solid, middle-aged woman who smelled faintly of cigarettes came right up behind them and at the pizza.

The woman plowed right through Sunset and Gail.

Sunset quickly pulled Gail aside, but not before they both knew the woman's full history, about her affair with an office worker, her divorce, about her inability to stop eating and smoking and gaining weight since the divorce, and how her two children really hated her for causing the divorce.

One romp in the hay had cost the woman everything she treasured and she had no idea how to even start to get it back.

That wasn't supposed to have happened. Not without Jewel here to train Gail.

Sunset put the plates they had been carrying down and took Gail's hand and led her back to the table.

Gail seemed to be in shock. He had to be careful, very careful to not be an idiot.

When they sat down, Sunset pushed the glass of water toward her. "Take a drink, it will help."

She did, then nodded. She came back into her eyes a little.

Then she looked up at him. "I'm not sure I want to see inside people's heads, into their lives, into their secrets."

Sunset nodded, thinking carefully, as if in a courtroom and every word mattered. And it really did. "I understand that. Thankfully, what we saw will fade quickly from our minds."

Silence.

Sunset let the silence go on as Gail worked over in her mind what had happened. He knew she was smart. He needed to trust her ability to think things through right now.

"This isn't really a dream, is it?" Gail asked after a long moment of staring at the heavy-set woman they knew so much about.

"No, it's not," he said.

"I'm really dead?" Gail asked, looking directly at him. "That accident on the highway really happened?"

"It did," Sunset said, his tone as gentle and understanding as he could make it. "But you now get a very rare chance of living an even better life, a very long life if you want, and help others at the same time."

She nodded.

Sunset couldn't think of one other thing to say. He really sucked at this training stuff.

Five

Once Gail accepted that she was dead, she wanted to know more about this crazy new world she found herself in. Part of her still didn't believe it, but for the moment she was going to just stop fighting it.

Sunset struggled a few times, in a very cute way, to try to explain a few things, and then looked massively relieved when Jewel and Tommy returned.

Damn he was cute.

Sunset asked them how it had gone and Jewel explained.

Gail was impressed that they had gotten the elderly couple to toss away the gun and call their children and tell them what was happening.

It seemed their children were very well off and had been worried about the couple. But the couple was too proud to say anything about not having any money left at all.

Gail was stunned at how Jewel and Tommy had literally saved lives. But Tommy had been a cop, Jewel a doctor. How did Gail being a prosecuting attorney help?

When she asked that question, Sunset had said that only time would tell. He had been an attorney as well and he had been doing fine.

So Gail had agreed to training with Jewel and Tommy, with Sunset helping every day, but taking only a supporting role.

Over the next month, Gail stayed in Jewel and Tommy's home in Las Vegas in their guest room and they trained in the casinos, helping people where they could.

Finally, after a month, as the four of them were eating breakfast back in the Golden Nugget Buffet, Jewel turned to Gail and said simply, "You ready to find your own place?"

Gail had known that was coming, but it worried her because she didn't know what she should do. She wanted to go back to Oregon, but she was fairly certain she didn't want to return to the coast. Portland was the only town she liked, but Sunset lived there and she didn't want to be too forward. They were both very attracted to each other, but so far during her training had kept arms distance.

And she was going to have to work with him, so having an affair with a partner might not be such a hot idea, even though she wanted to. She had a hunch they would decide that later.

Gail pushed her waffle away and sat back.

Jewel just smiled and Tommy kept eating.

"I own this wonderful penthouse condo in Portland that

is just sitting empty," Sunset said. "You can have it if you would like."

"You own it?" Gail asked. "How do you do that?"

"Actually a corporation I formed owns it," Sunset said. "I'll explain how all that is possible someday down the road on a really long and boring day."

"And you are willing to give the condo to me?" Gail asked.

"No problem," Sunset said, shrugging. "Money is never much of an issue for us ghosts, you know."

Sunset turned to Jewel. "Could you get some of your superhero friends to move some real furniture into the place. Furniture Gail picks out if she wants to take it?"

"Glad to," Jewel said, smiling.

Gail smiled at Jewel. "Thanks."

She couldn't believe how lucky she felt right now to be with these three wonderful people. And to have this exciting new life ahead of her, even though she was actually dead. She felt alive, more than she had ever felt when actually living.

Then Gail looked back at Sunset, her future partner, who was smiling. "That's very kind of you and I accept. Thank you."

Sunset nodded.

Gail turned back to Jewel. "Does this mean I'm done with my training?"

"Sunset can take it from here," Jewel said. "But we'll always be here if you need us for anything. We all work together you know."

Gail nodded.

"One condition to all this," Sunset said, smiling at her.

"Once you are all moved in, you throw a party. I'll make the tequila sunsets."

"You're damn lucky I love that drink," Gail said, laughing.

"Yeah," Sunset said, "I think I am."

Gail pulled her waffle back toward her and took another bite, savoring the rich maple syrup flavor.

Around her the wonderful sounds of the morning in the Golden Nugget Buffet went on.

People talking. People laughing.

People being alive.

She hadn't planned to die on that highway on her way to dinner a month ago.

No one expects to die.

But now, sitting here with other Ghost Agents in a restaurant full of the living that she knew she might be able to help if they needed it, dying didn't seem so bad.

And sitting beside Sunset just made it all the better.

Oh wow did it make it better.

She had to die to meet the man of her dreams. She had a hunch it was going to be worth it.

PART TWO

A First Big Job

Six

The wildest five months Gail could ever have imagined had just passed. Now she sat at her kitchen table in her beautiful condo overlooking downtown Portland and watched as Sunset scanned through his morning news on an iPad sitting on the kitchen table.

She was still learning to make her touch firm enough to control a computer or even move something on a table. Every day she felt she got closer. Sunset had told her that things took time to learn. After all, she had only been dead five months.

Hard to believe that just five months ago she had been a successful prosecuting attorney on the Oregon Coast. Before her wonderful red BMV lost an unfair fight with a large truck.

Just as with every morning, Sunset looked like he had come right out of court and had just taken off his tie. He always wore a dark suit made of silk and a silk shirt. Plus he always wore perfectly polished expensive shoes. He dressed the same every morning and she sort of liked that about him. He was, by far, the most handsome man Gail had ever seen.

She was dressed in what made her feel comfortable. Dark dress slacks, comfortable matching shoes with short heels, a silk blouse and silk bra under it.

She and Sunset made a perfect power couple, but so far they were just partners even though she was flat out in lust with him.

She watched him work at the computer for a moment longer, then turned to stare out the large windows. Outside her wonderful penthouse condo, the Portland skies were gray. The fall had been beautiful, but now heading into November the season was changing, the air getting a bite to it, and the leaves on the trees turning stunning shades of orange, red, and brown.

She actually loved the fall and winter in Oregon. This was going to be her first winter as a ghost, so she didn't know what to expect, exactly.

Sunset, when he had been alive, had been a lawyer in private practice and had spent a lot of time in the last decade helping out in poor areas and giving free legal advice at a clinic in the northeast side of Portland.

He had died over a hundred years ago in a boating accident on the Willamette River. As he had freely told her, he had had one too many tequila sunsets and he had fallen out and hit his head on the side of the boat.

He said he sat on the bank for an hour watching them search for his body after trying to wave them down before he realized he was a ghost. No one had been there the moment he died as he and three other Ghost Agents had been for her. It wasn't until an hour later that someone from the Ghost of a Chance agency showed up and tried to start explaining things.

As Sunset said, they didn't get off well together right from the start.

Gail, on the other hand had been met the moment she died in the car wreck by Jewel and Tommy and K.J. and Sunset and then trained. Where Sunset had learned most things himself about being a Ghost Agent, Gail couldn't imagine doing that.

So, now as a ghost for the hundred-plus years, Sunset had tried to help those that seemed to need some help. When Gail asked him his record, he shrugged. "Some are beyond help."

The condo they were in was owned by a corporation that Sunset had started. He had done that by going inside the body of a live lawyer and getting the lawyer to do the work, then clearing out any memory of what that lawyer had done.

And not leaving any record of the lawyer on the documents either.

Sunset had learned to be an expert in computers and legal issues involving computers and how to leave no trail. Gail had a hunch she hadn't seen the level of his expertise yet. She had asked him about it once and he had laughed and said, "When you have been around as long as I have, you get ahead of the new stuff coming in."

Sunset had hired a "record firm" to be the address of record for the corporation who owned this condo and other properties around town, again just going inside a person in the firm to set it up.

Money to buy this condo and others had come easily from a few scams that he had busted. He drained the accounts of the bad guys and made sure that the money could never be traced out of the country and then back into his corporation. He used the money to buy land and places like this condo he had given her. Often with the land and buildings he bought he lowered the rent for social services, trying to help them out.

Gail had been stunned over and over the last few months at how Sunset, who had come off brash and pushy at first, spent most of his days trying to figure out ways to help others.

After her training, they had taken to meeting every morning in her place to plan the day. So far, they both had managed to hold the physical part of the relationship at bay, but she wanted to change that and change that soon. Who knew a ghost could get so horny?

Being a ghost and being able to be inside a live person had been one of the more stunning things Gail had learned. At first she hated it, but as her training had gone on, she got good at directing a live person and sometimes helping them.

And, of course, the live person never knew Gail was there.

"So how about we tackle something larger today?" Sunset said, staring at the iPad. "Now that there are two of us, we might be able to."

"What are you thinking?" she asked, moving over and putting her hand on his shoulder and leaning down to see the screen better. She loved touching Sunset and she loved when Sunset touched her as well.

She pushed the thought aside about taking him into the bedroom and focused on the computer screen in front of her.

"Out in Gresham there's an investment firm that is starting to get complaints," Sunset said, pointing to an article. "Got a hunch they might be thinking of covering their tracks here shortly if we don't do something to help out the police."

Gail smiled. "White collar crime. That's my favorite type."

He laughed. "Me too.

"Let's go see what we can see," she said, looking at the address of the main office. "You want me to jump us there or you want to do it?"

"I don't think you need the practice, but what the hell, go ahead," Sunset said.

She took his hand and a moment later they were standing to one side of a fairly busy office on the main floor of the three-story building. The office was bright and had large windows along one wall. Doors into smaller offices lined the far wall and one sidewall. Twenty desks with cubical walls around them filled the space, all with a person at the desk behind a computer, talking with someone on the phone over a headset.

They all looked relaxed and busy.

The place didn't feel like it had just had a negative article written about it. It felt like an active business on just a normal day.

"Did I get us to the right spot?" Gail asked, glancing

around as two people walked by, laughing at some conversation.

Sunset nodded. "This is the right spot but this is not at all what I was expecting. Not at all."

She could only agree with that. Something was wrong. Very, very wrong.

Seven

Sunset felt stunned at the big office in front of them. This place should be a stress-filled office with workers huddled whispering and panicked looks on manager's faces. That article this morning in the paper had been damaging to say the least and would be fatal to a business playing a scam as this one clearly was.

But nothing seemed to be wrong here. Maybe the article had just been a revenge piece from someone who had lost money here. But it hadn't felt that way. It had been done by a major reporter for the paper and clearly had the backing of the editors of the paper.

In his years as a live attorney, or his years as a Ghost Agent, Sunset had seen the pattern of a scam investment company numbers of times once the rock they had been hiding under was lifted. They fled like bugs afraid of the light.

No one in this room was fleeing or even seeming to be worried about their job or the company they worked for.

"This is off," he said to Gail.

"Way, way off," Gail said, nodding.

Over the last five months, Sunset had come to really respect Gail's opinions. She was smart, more than likely smarter than he was about many things. And she was the best-looking woman he had ever met. They were just settling into working together, but what he really wanted was for them to take the partnership to a relationship.

And soon.

Real soon.

Across the room was a guy in an expensive gray suit without a tie smiling at some other manager type.

"I'm going to see what he is thinking," Sunset said, pointing to the expensive suit.

Gail nodded. "I'll see what the brunette here at this first desk is worried about."

Sunset jumped over beside the guy in the suit and merged inside of him, making sure to be very careful that the guy didn't know Sunset had joined him in any fashion. Most people didn't notice when a ghost was riding along in their minds, but a few, a very few, could sense something different.

Sunset didn't need to worry about this guy. His mind was mostly a blank slate. His entire focus was to sell the many forms of securities this company was selling. And he really, really believed that this company was helping people.

Sunset stayed inside the guy's mind. It felt as off as the entire office felt. Almost as if Sunset was inside an empty gym. Most people's minds were full of a thousand thoughts, all jumbled.

In this guy, all that was gone.

Slowly, digging back into the guy's past, working through memories of his wife and kids, Sunset finally found what he feared.

This guy had been run through a therapy brainwashing system of some sort. It had been quick and complete, of that there was no doubt.

Sunset eased out of the guy and jumped back to where Gail had gone inside the brunette sitting in front of one of the desks.

After a moment Gail appeared, looking shocked.

And angry.

In the few short months, Sunset had never seen Gail angry and he had a hunch she would be a power to get out of the way of when she did get angry.

"The poor thing was brainwashed," Gail said. "So much so that she left her boyfriend of three years, moved in with two other women working here, and all they talk about is how fantastic this work is."

"So was the boss," Sunset said.

"We have to figure out how far this spreads," Gail said.

Sunset agreed completely. They quickly split up the building. She would take the rest of the main floor, going into random people to see what was going on with them, he would go to the second floor and check that. They would meet near the elevator on the second floor and both check out the top floor at the same time, where they expected the bosses to be.

Thirty minutes later they stood in front of the president of the company's office. He had been as brainwashed as everyone else in the entire building.

That fact had shocked Sunset more than he wanted to admit.

The big evil of this place didn't work here.

"So now what do we do?" Gail asked, shaking her head. Sunset could see anger was clearly still there

Sunset was angry as well, but it was covered by a feeling of sadness for the almost two hundred people in this building.

Sunset looked at Gail. "We need lunch, then we need a lot more research on this company."

"How about we do a little research before lunch?" Gail said. "How about we go visit that reporter who wrote the article this morning, see what he has already dug up."

Sunset smiled. "Really, really good idea."

This time he took her hand, something he loved doing, and jumped them both to the reporter's office on the second floor of the city's major newspaper.

Eight

Gail was barely controlling the anger she felt at how all those people were being controlled.

And being used to hurt other people.

Whoever was behind this was the scum of the earth. And in Gail's training, Jewel had shown Gail a few tricks to make the really ugly people suffer. Gail just hoped she remembered a few of those when she met the person or people who were behind this.

The reporter was a solid man, about forty, with a beer gut. He wore jeans and a plain T-shirt and a Cubs baseball cap that more than likely covered a bald spot.

His office was a messy control center and when they arrived he was sitting behind his computer, typing.

They both nodded to each other and went inside him together, still holding hands.

The guy's name was Ryan and he was a bubbling mass of

anger. The article he was working on was about the company they had just visited, about how much money the company scam had taken for worthless property and investments. All from innocent investors who bought into the sales line.

The guy had really done his research. The company in Oregon was nothing more than a shell company. All the money came in and vanished into overseas accounts. And his article had done nothing at all to dent their business and that was why he was angry.

He wanted to take them down and hard and fast.

Gail agreed with that completely.

His focus on the new article he was writing was the investors, warning them away, trying to convince them to sell their investments and try to get some of their money back.

Sunset had no real hope anyone would get any money back. In fact, he knew, without a doubt, this one was within one week of shutting down. That was the pattern.

But in one week a lot of people could and would still be hurt.

The reporter flat didn't understand why even the president of the company was just giving him the company line, even though there was a chance the guy would end up in prison.

Gail knew. Everyone, including the president had been brainwashed in such an effective manner as to be frightening. Every person in that building totally believed to their core they were doing good for people and their money.

Gail and Sunset stepped out of the reporter's body and then Sunset jumped them to a wonderful deli-style restaurant in the Pearl District. They grabbed a few ghost sandwiches a couple of customers had ordered and then jumped back to her condo to eat at the table, since the weather was too cold to eat out on the deli's outside space.

She got some plates and bottles of water. Then they ate in silence for a few minutes, both thinking. She liked that about being with Sunset. He had no problem with silence.

Finally she looked at him and asked the question she didn't know the answer to.

"Think we can clear their minds?"

Sunset nodded. "One at a time," he said, "but we can do it."

"How?" she asked.

"We go into their minds and simply wipe out the few hours of brainwashing sessions. We erase it."

Gail was shocked. "We can erase someone's memories? Jewel never said a word about being able to do that."

Sunset nodded, looking slightly pained. "I learned how to do it with a rape survivor who couldn't stop wanting to kill herself. The memories she had were so vivid, it was as if she was living them again and again every day. I finally went in and not only dulled the memories, but erased most of them. It gave the poor kid a chance to find a way to recover."

Gail nodded, not wanting to imagine how hard that must have been for Sunset to do.

"So you can show me how?" she asked.

Sunset nodded. "But I am suggesting we erase not only the memories of the brainwashing, but the memories of the months working for the company. The longest is about five months that I saw."

"That would leave a big hole in all their lives," Gail said, stunned that he suggested that.

Sunset nodded. "Better that than those poor people living with the guilt of what they did to others. Suicide would be a choice a number of them would make with that kind of guilt."

Damn, he was right. It would be better to have a person just sort of wake up and learn about what they had been doing from others than remember it and regret it deeply.

She and Sunset finished their sandwiches, talking over the plan of how to cover the entire building. They were both worried about how bosses would react, how workers would react, and how the people they hadn't gotten to yet would deal with others suddenly stopping what they were doing. There were over two hundred people in that building and there just was no way to clear them all quickly.

And Gail had no doubt they couldn't do it before five when everyone went home.

Finally, Gail said simply, "We can't do this alone. We need help."

Sunset nodded, clearly agreeing.

Gail sort of looked up at the ceiling, focusing on the two that had trained her and said, "Jewel? Tommy? We need your help."

She and Sunset had gotten into a case too big for them to deal with in the first few months of their partnership.

Didn't that just figure?

Nine

Sunset really had come to like and admire Jewel and Tommy during Gail's training. And the four of them had had a lot of fun meals together over the months as well.

Jewel and Tommy appeared in just moments after Gail asked for them. Both of them were wearing their normal jeans and dress shirts and running shoes. Tommy kept his dark brown hair cut short and Jewel had her brown hair pulled back as she seemed to always do.

They had quickly proven to the powers running everything that they were the best at what they did. Sunset had learned some things from them as well during Gail's training.

"You guys ever not dress up?" Tommy asked.

Sunset glanced at Gail's business suit and then at his own silk suit.

"Our working clothes," Gail said, smiling.

Tommy had teased them about how they always looked like they were fresh out of court. Sunset didn't mind. It made him feel comfortable.

"Problems?" Jewel asked.

Sunset indicated that Gail explain what they had found. And what they needed help doing.

When she was done, Jewel looked at Sunset. "You can cut out that much memory permanently from a person?"

"I can," Sunset said, nodding. "I can show you how. Some of these people will be dealing with doctors and such trying to regain their memory of the months, but they never will."

"We figure that would be better than the guilt they will experience," Gail said. "This financial scam has hurt thousands, will take many families entire savings. I would have trouble living with a memory of doing that to anyone."

Jewel and Tommy both nodded.

Sunset was glad they agreed.

"No sign of who is in charge?" Tommy asked.

"Going to be spending a lot of time on digging out that worm," Sunset said, "once we stop this and stop more people from getting hurt. But the reporter who dug all this up knows that the money is vanishing into overseas accounts. He just can't confirm that yet."

"So the key right now is stopping this," Jewel said. "Lay out your plan for us."

"We clear the brainwashing of the officers and board members and upper management, but leave the memories," Gail said. "They will be able to help prosecutors and also, more than likely, end up in jail. At least they will know why they are there."

Sunset nodded. "The rest of them we go in and just cut out everything that happened from the moment they were put under control of whoever is doing this to the present."

Jewel and Tommy nodded.

"I have one question," Sunset said. "You ever hear of anyone being able to do this kind of mind control at this level?"

"Besides one of us when we are inside someone," Jewel said. "No. But when we are finished I will ask some of the superheroes if they have heard of such a thing."

Sunset was afraid of that. "We will be researching that after we get this done. So anything from any of these victims that we can get today as to how this was done will help as well."

They all nodded. Sunset doubted they would find anything. Of the people whose minds he had been in, the brainwashing had happened seemingly instantly as they sat in front of a computer screen answering a few basic questions.

Something on that screen had gotten to them, implanted this belief about this scam company being the greatest. More than likely the people really behind this scam weren't even in this country.

They certainly weren't in that building.

Eventually, they would be found, but that wasn't going to be today. Today they had to stop this cancer right here in Portland.

"Be careful around that moment of brainwashing," Gail said. "We don't want any of us getting hit with it."

Sunset and Jewel and Tommy all nodded to that as well and until one in the afternoon, when employees would be returning from lunch, the four of them planned their attack on the two-hundred-plus people in the three-story building.

Ten

Gail felt terrified at what they were about to do.

All four of them jumped to a back room on the lower floor of the building and all four of them went into one poor man's head.

He was a mailroom guy named Stanley who was fresh out of an MBA degree. He had only been working for the company for a month. His goal was to work his way up in this fantastic company and maybe someday own stock in it as well.

Sunset quickly, using this guy as an example, showed Gail and Jewel and Tommy how he removed a section of the man's memory.

Gail was surprised at how simple it was. Sunset simply put a clear mental box around the memory and then just shrunk the space inside the box until the box was nothing more than a dot.

Instantly the guy seemed confused as to where he was and what he had been doing.

Sunset gave him some calming thoughts and told him to just go home.

Then Jewel and Tommy and Sunset and Gail left the guy's mind as the poor MBA grad left the building.

"We're going to have to plant some memories," Jewel said, "in people as to where they parked their car, where they live if they moved while working here, things like that."

"And calming thoughts," Gail said. "I want to try to keep these people calm because it's going to feel like they are just waking up."

All three of them nodded to her suggestion. That would take them all more time, but it would be worth it for the people they were saving.

"So here we go," Sunset said. "Let's get the officers first. Just clear the brainwashing in the same way. A mental box around only the time they were at that computer, squeeze it down to nothing."

Gail took a deep breath and a moment later they were walking into the plush offices on the third floor.

It took the four of them about thirty minutes to clear the brainwashing from the officers and then erase the memories of the support staff working upstairs. Gail dealt with two women who had been with the company since the start. She calmed them as much as she could and gave them the suggestion to just get their coat and things and leave.

Then Gail and Sunset and Jewel and Tommy went to the second floor.

They started with the managers first, then worked their way through each room. In one hour they had that floor cleared.

The ground floor was looking a little frightened as everyone upstairs seemed to be going out the front door, looking confused.

Again the four of them started with the managers of the room and by four in the afternoon, the building seemed empty.

Gail had so many people's memories and thoughts in her head, she felt a little confused herself. But a few deep breaths and things seemed to sort out some.

The four of them had done it before five.

They spent the next thirty minutes making sure they hadn't missed anyone. By that point, Gail felt a lot better. The only people left in the building were the officers of the company upstairs, huddling together, talking about what they should do.

One man was just sitting in his office crying.

Gail hated to see that and pointed the guy out to Sunset who went into the crying man and a moment later the guy stopped, stood, squared his shoulders, and went to talk with the other officers.

"I just gave the guy a backbone is all," Sunset said, smiling at Gail as he appeared next to her.

"I'm going to go tell the reporter to check the building now," Sunset said. "Maybe contact the officers. You guys up for dinner?"

"I'm sort of missing the buffet dinner at the Golden

Nugget in Vegas," Gail said. That was the restaurant that the four of them had eaten in the most during her months of training.

And today, this had felt like a lot more training.

"Wonderful idea," Sunset said, smiling at her. "I'll meet you all there."

He vanished.

"Great by us," Jewel said.

Jewel and Tommy smiled and vanished.

Gail stopped and looked around the now empty main room full of desks and computers. The four of them had saved a lot of people a lot of grief and lost money this afternoon.

They had shut down a scam. As a prosecuting attorney, that had always felt good to her.

She had been dead now for five months. And as each day went by, she felt more and more useful.

And that felt wonderful.

She nodded to the empty room and jumped to join her friends and the man she was head-over-heels in lust with.

Maybe after a good dinner in Las Vegas, she and Sunset could come back to her apartment, have a few drinks, watch a movie, and then end up in her big bed in celebration of a job well done.

She would like that.

Far more than she wanted to think about before dinner.

Eleven

Sunset woke up next to Gail in her huge bed. The light from the late fall sunrise was flowing in through her bedroom window and in the distance he could see the cars crossing one of the many Portland bridges.

Beside him she lay sprawled, her normally perfectly-combed brown hair sticking out in all directions. Her face was so beautiful, he could stare at her all day and never get tired of it. He loved her pointed yet short nose, her thin eyebrows that seemed to express her every emotion, and that small mouth, still red from all the kissing last night.

Her wonderful body was half-exposed and she looked like a goddess. How in the world had he gotten so lucky after a hundred years of being dead.

They had finally taken their partnership to a relationship last night and it had been better than he had even imagined it might be. And for the last five months, since first seeing her, his imagination had been very active.

But they just seemed to fit together in all ways and all likes.

As he stared at her, she stirred and opened one eye. Then she closed her eye and sighed.

"Damn, glad that wasn't a dream."

"You have dreams like that?" he asked.

She smiled. "About you, I had a few like that, only not that good. And don't let that go to your head."

He laughed and kissed her and she turned and moved into his arms.

And once again they just sort of fit together.

In all ways.

Thirty minutes later he finally crawled out of the bed and headed for the shower, leaving her sprawled naked on the bed. That was an image he would not ever be able to forget, he had no doubt about that.

She joined him in the bathroom as he was drying off. She kissed him with a smile and then, without a word, got into the shower.

"I'll get coffee," he said.

"Oh, that would be heaven," she said.

"I think I'm already in heaven," he said, laughing.

"Yeah, thinking the same thing," she said.

Thirty minutes later they were both dressed and sipping on their coffee and eating slices of toast while Sunset pulled up the story on the investment firm in the paper. It was the lead article.

And as they both knew, none of the officers had any idea what had happened or who was behind the company. And the reporter agreed with them. And until someone figured out where all the money had gone to in the scam, none of the investors were going to get much if anything back.

"Seems we know what we need to do next," Sunset said.

"Find the worm behind all that," Gail said.

"And find out how they brainwashed all those people," Sunset said. "That has me the most worried. I can't imagine that anyone smart enough to do this would leave evidence on any computer. So it had to come in over the cloud somehow."

Gail nodded. "I noticed the program the people were watching when the brainwashing happened. It was a company orientation video they had to log on to get."

"Yeah, saw the same thing," Sunset said.

"You know anyone good enough to trace something like that back to a source? If it would be even possible."

Sunset smiled at her and nodded. "I'm not sure it is possible, but if it is, it's going to take pulling some strings for us to find someone good enough to do it."

"You know someone like that?"

He nodded. He didn't really know the person, but had heard rumors as computers became a thing over the last thirty years. The best there was, the actual god of computers and programming. And all the good and bad that went along with them.

But he had never met a god or even much realized the gods existed until just lately. He had always thought this person, called a god, to be a rumor. Now he wasn't so sure.

But it might be the best shot. The skill to trace something like this was far beyond his abilities, he knew that for sure.

Gail just stared at him like he had lost a marble. "Not some kid we just take over, huh?"

Sunset laughed. "Nope, on something like this we need the best."

"And the best is?"

"From what I have heard, she used to go by the name Pheme," Sunset said. "Not a clue what name she is using these days. But I think a friend of Jewel and Tommy's might be able to help."

"Pheme as in fame?"

"Spelled with a ph and an e," Sunset said. "Again, all rumor, but lately I'm starting to think some of these rumors actually exist."

Gail nodded. "Strange name."

Sunset just laughed. "From what I have heard, that's only the start of it."

Twelve

⁶◦○◦⁹

G ail loved the fact that she and Sunset had finally taken their partnership and flirting to a relation-ship. It felt right, felt comfortable, and had been an amazing amount of fun, both last night and this morning when they woke up.

And now, from the sounds of it, they were off on an adventure to find someone to help them track that mind-altering program those poor people at the company had been subjected to.

"You want me to call Jewel and Tommy?" Gail asked.

They had both finished their coffee and toast and had finished reading the morning articles about the scam they had broken up yesterday.

Outside the penthouse windows the morning sun was breaking through the clouds, promising a nice fall day in Portland.

"Please," Sunset said.

Gail focused on Jewel and Tommy and called their names. The she said, "Need a little help when you have a minute."

Less than a minute later Jewel and Tommy both appeared. Gail knew that at this time of the day in Las Vegas, they both would have been eating breakfast at the Golden Nugget buffet. They would have already done their morning runs and then showered.

They were very much people of schedule.

"Sorry for the interruption," Gail said to them after Sunset offered Jewel and Tommy coffee and they both shook their heads. "We think we might need a little help tracing the computer program back to a source."

"We figured as much," Jewel said, smiling. She turned to Sunset. "You thinking of trying to find Pheme?"

Sunset nodded. "I'm only guessing she actually exists. But if she does, her reputation tells me she might have a chance of tracing something like that through just about anything. I did a little work yesterday after I cleared one person who was pretty good at computers. I had him try to trace back the training program. It didn't exist on his or any computer in that firm. Or on the firm's cloud storage in any form."

Gail was impressed that Sunset had done that. She had tried a little of the same, but didn't get as far as he had.

"So it didn't really exist," Tommy said. "But it came from somewhere? I got the same results when I tried to have someone trace it yesterday."

"Exactly," Sunset said.

"We have already called Poker Boy," Jewel said. "He and a couple of his team are waiting for us in his office."

Gail looked at Sunset who was nodding, then at Jewel and Tommy. She had no idea what kind of name Poker Boy was, but that was the second time in her five months of being dead she had heard the name. Looked like she was about to find out.

"Never been there or met him," Sunset said. "So do the honors and jump us there."

Jewel nodded and a moment later Gail found herself standing in one of the strangest offices she had ever seen. It was basically a square with windows for walls on all four sides and a glass ceiling. The only furniture in the entire room was a huge booth that looked like it was right out of a 1950s diner. Red leather bench seats around three sides, a scarred Formica tabletop, and a few wooden chairs scattered around the open end.

Outside the glass walls it was clear the room was floating a thousand feet in the air right over the Las Vegas strip. A large airliner making an approach to the airport went past far too close for Gail's tastes.

Not possible.

This room wasn't possible. It must be some sort of illusion.

A wooden railing at waist high went all the way around the room, otherwise Gail would have felt she would slip on the checkered tile floor and fall off of the office.

She forced herself to take a deep breath and try to just look around.

The morning outside those windows was stunning. The air clear, the mountains in the distance on three sides sharp and looking like they were very close. Jaw-dropping view and she bet her mouth was open at the moment staring.

Beside her Sunset's mouth was open as he stared out of the windows as well.

"Jewel, Tommy," a voice said from behind them.

Sunset and Gail turned around to see Tommy and Jewel hugging a guy in a black leather coat, jeans, and a black fedora-like hat. The guy seemed to be about the same age as the rest of them with a smile that could charm an entire room.

Behind him a stunning woman with long brown hair and wearing an MGM Grand uniform slid out of the booth, also smiling.

Staying in the booth was a guy in a gray cardigan sweater and an older guy who looked like anyone's classic grandfather, right down to the wire-rimmed glasses perched on his nose.

The woman hugged both Jewel and Tommy, then Jewel did the honors of the introductions.

"This is Gail and Sunset," Jewel said.

Jewel indicated the guy with the hat and black leather coat. "This is Poker Boy."

He nodded and smiled.

"This is Patty, aka Front Desk Girl."

She smiled and nodded at both of them.

"In the sweater is Stan, the God of Poker and beside him is Ben, the God of Libraries."

Gail wanted to open her mouth and ask about a dozen stupid questions, but for the moment she decided to just wait and ask later. If she hadn't been dead and standing in a glass office floating a thousand feet above Las Vegas, she might have questioned the idea she was meeting gods.

But she had been dead now for five months and so far every day had surprised her. Today was just a little larger surprise than most.

"Join us," Poker Boy said, indicating the booth. "You two just came from court or something?"

"That is how they always dress," Tommy said.

"Best dressed people ever to see this dump," Poker Boy said, shaking his head.

They all moved toward the booth as Poker Boy said to Sunset, "Heard a lot of good things about you since someone filled me in on the Ghost of a Chance agents."

"Thanks," Sunset said. "I didn't know all of you existed until a few years ago and since then heard nothing but good about you and your team."

Patty touched Gail's shoulder as she and Sunset took a seat facing the booth and Jewel and Tommy scooted into the booth after Stan and Sunset moved farther in.

With Patty's touch Gail felt much calmer. Clearly some sort of power or magic. Either way, Gail appreciated it and nodded thanks to Patty.

"Sorry to hear about your accident," Patty said. "But very glad you could join the team and work with Sunset."

"Thank you," Gail said. "It's been an adventure so far."

Gail was actually more stunned at Patty's mentioning of

the accident. Not a person had mentioned it before that moment and Gail had honestly spent no time thinking about it or her lost life on the coast. No grief, nothing.

She found that odd, now that she thought about it. She would have to ask Sunset about that later.

"So how can we help you?" Poker Boy asked.

Sunset and Jewel took turns explaining about the scam company and what they had found and about the brainwashing program that vanished from the computers.

"So you really can erase areas of a person's memory?" Patty asked.

"Only if we have to in order to keep the person either sane or alive," Sunset said. "But yes, we can and we had to do it in this case. Both to get rid of the brainwashing and to help them through the recovery."

Jewel and Tommy were both nodding.

"Wow," Poker Boy said, nodding. "That's a skill that might come in real handy at times."

"So you want to find a way to trace that program back to the source?" Stan asked.

Sunset nodded. "We're thinking Pheme might be able to help."

"Who?" Poker Boy asked.

Ben had sat back, shaking his head and closing his eyes. Stan just looked like a frozen statue.

"Oh, shit," Patty said softly.

Gail just looked at the reaction among the gods and Poker Boy's puzzled look. This clearly might not be a good idea.

Not good at all.

Thirteen

❧

S unset was stunned at the reaction of the team of gods. He had heard that Pheme was a problem, but not one that would cause these kinds of reactions.

"Okay," Poker Boy said, clearly not happy. "Who is this Pheme and why the reaction?"

Stan just shook his head. Then he said simply, "Laverne?"

A moment later a thin woman in a silk blue pants suit and a white blouse appeared. She had her dark brown hair pulled back tight off her face, giving her a stark and commanding look.

Sunset immediately stood and stepped back, pulling the stunned Gail with him as he went. He had no idea how he managed to stay on his feet, but he did.

The woman smiled and stuck out her hand toward him. "Sunset, wonderful to meet you finally after all these years."

Sunset shook Laverne's hand. He couldn't believe he was

actually shaking the hand of Lady Luck herself, the most powerful god among all gods, the god who ran everything.

He was so stunned he couldn't even get a word out.

Laverne didn't seem to notice. She turned to Gail. "Welcome to the other side of things, Gail. I'm Laverne."

Gail nodded and said, "Wonderful to meet you."

Laverne laughed, then glanced at Sunset. "She has no idea who I am, does she?"

Sunset smiled. "Not a clue."

"Explain it to her later," Laverne said, smiling. "Come on and sit back down. Madge is bringing up fries and some shakes."

Sunset managed to get Gail back to their chairs and make room for Lady Luck to sit beside them. Somehow he managed that without tripping over a chair or shaking too much.

After all, it was Lady Luck who had just joined them.

A moment later a woman five sizes too large in all ways for her 1950s waitress uniform appeared from behind the booth and served them all milkshakes and the most fantastic-smelling French fries he had ever seen.

"I'm Madge," the woman said to Sunset and Gail as she slid the fries in front of everyone and then put a massive chocolate milkshake in a tall, heavy glass in front of them.

"I figured you two could split one to start with," Madge said. "But if you want more, just shout."

"Thanks, Madge," Laverne said as the large woman moved around behind the booth and went through a door there.

Sunset had no idea where a door would lead considering

they were in a room floating high above Las Vegas, but it had to go somewhere.

"So," Poker Boy said, "the ghost crew here thinks a person by the name of Pheme might be able to help them trace a computer problem. I have no idea who that is."

Laverne munched on a fry and nodded. "If anyone can trace anything through computer networks of any kind, real or magical, Pheme can do it. But she doesn't go by Pheme anymore. She has been Dottie now for centuries."

"So these three had a reaction when the name Pheme was mentioned," Poker Boy said. "And then they called you. What has she done to cause that?"

Lady Luck smiled and Sunset could feel it. He had a hunch people down on the Strip below could feel it. And the smile was a fond one.

"Pheme has a reputation of being wild and going her own way," Lady Luck said. "That's all."

The old man named Ben just shook his head and looked down at the fries in front of him.

Stan, the God of Poker, actually smiled.

Sunset had a hunch Laverne was glossing over some of the issues with Pheme, or Dottie, or whatever she was now called.

"Have you seen Pheme lately?" Patty asked.

Laverne again smiled and her gaze got distant. Again it was a warm and fond smile. "We meet every Tuesday for lunch."

Silence filled the office and no one said a word around the booth as Laverne sat there, a distant look in her eyes, a fond smile on her face. If Sunset had to guess, Laverne and Dottie were doing more than having lunch every week.

But no way in hell was he going to ask Lady Luck a question like that.

Nope.

Not a chance.

No damn way.

Fourteen

G ail was completely startled by Sunset's response when the attractive, thin woman in the silk suit appeared. Clearly the woman was powerful, but she also seemed very nice.

So far today, Gail had met five very nice people, or gods, or whatever they were, and one waitress who really should be pulled aside and talked to about how to pick clothes that fit.

And now it was clear that this woman by the name of Laverne and Pheme, or Dottie, were very close. More than likely affair close. And it seemed that everyone but Poker Boy and she and Sunset had known that.

"So do you think Dottie can help these agents get a trace on this scammer?" Poker Boy asked.

Laverne shrugged, still smiling. "Let's ask her. Dottie, could you join us for a moment?"

A second later a very short, thin woman who looked to be

about thirty appeared next to Laverne. She had short blonde hair that was clearly styled and wore jeans, tennis shoes, and a tan blouse that had an Apple Computers logo on it.

"Was just going to take a break," the woman said. She smiled at the table. "Great finally meeting all of you. I'm Dottie."

Laverne went quickly around the table doing introductions, then when she got to the four Ghost Agents, Dottie got very excited.

"Always heard rumors there was a ghost crew working on helping people," Dottie said. "Great to finally meet some of you."

"The pleasure is ours," Jewel said, smiling.

"Pull up a chair and grab a fry," Laverne said. "They have a favor to ask of you."

"Oh, fun," Dottie said, bringing a chair up beside Laverne.

Gail could tell that Laverne and Dottie were clearly very close just by how they sat touching shoulders.

Jewel quickly told Dottie the story of the scam and how they had saved the people in the building but couldn't trace the program. The entire time Dottie sat munching on some fries.

Gail hadn't touched the fries or the milkshake in front of her and neither had Sunset. She didn't feel like eating at the moment.

"Wow," Dottie said. "That's a damned dangerous program."

Everyone at the table nodded, including Laverne.

"I'm fairly sure I can trace the program back through

whatever it bounced through," Dottie said. "But what we find on the other side has me a lot worried."

"That kind of programming could be used for all sorts of things," Laverne said, nodding. "From suicide defenders to forms of brainwashing anyone who comes at the people behind this."

"No protection against anything like this?" Poker Boy asked.

"It's been a while since anything like this," Laverne said. "Ben, have you any ideas?"

The older-looking god shook his head. "Rumors of something like it still existing back in the Atlantis days. Used on criminals."

"Of course," Laverne said as both she and Dottie nodded at the same time. "The Necklace Stone."

Gail did not much like the sound of that and around the table everyone frowned.

"Haven't seen old H in decades," Dottie said.

"She's here in Vegas," Laverne said.

"No shit," Dottie said, taking another fry. "She working as a hooker?"

Laverne laughed, but she was the only one. The rest of them just sat silent.

Gail could tell instantly there was bad blood between Dottie and whoever the "H" person was.

"No," Laverne said, "she actually is working as a counselor at a local high school and going by the name of Harmony."

"Well good for her," Dottie said, still munching on a fry.

Laverne turned to the four Ghost Agents. "I have a hunch it might be better if you four approached Harmony."

Dottie laughed and kept eating.

Gail was certain that Laverne was right about that. But she had no desire to meet someone these two women were feuding with.

"For fear of asking one of my amazingly stupid questions," Poker Boy said, "any chance the rest of us can be filled in."

"Ancient history," Dottie said.

Laverne said nothing, clearly answering Poker Boy's question.

At that point Dottie looked directly at the four Ghost Agents and said, "When you need me to track that program, just shout my name. But first find out what happened to that necklace. You need to see if we can use it for protection or not, and then we need to figure out exactly what we are dealing with."

Then Dottie smiled at Laverne. "Thanks for the fries. My break is almost over. Got to get back to work. See you Tuesday?"

Laverne smiled and nodded. "Tuesday it is."

"Call me when you are ready," Dottie said to the four Ghost Agents.

And Dottie was gone.

All Gail could do was sit and stare at where she had been. And wonder exactly what the hell was going on.

Fifteen

Sunset sat silent along with everyone else for a moment after Dottie vanished. He was as confused as everyone seemed to be at the moment. They had come to find help with a computer trace and ended up seemingly in the middle of something larger and much older.

"Ben," Laverne said. "Explain to everyone what they are facing and dealing with if it is the Necklace Stone and what it protects against."

The older man at the table nodded and Laverne vanished.

"Well, that was interesting," Poker Boy said. He grabbed a fry and looked at Ben. "How long a story is this going to be?"

Ben shook his head. "Not long, actually. The Necklace Stone they are talking about didn't start off to be a necklace. It was a crystal, blue and green in hue, and about three inches long. It actually was an ancient technology we got from the

Titans in that war. It had the capability to block the control of minds."

"So it was magic?" Sunset asked.

"No," Ben said, shaking his head. "Magic only exists in the dark form. Computers and televisions would look like magic to someone from just a few hundred years ago. This crystal was actually an advanced ancient alien technology."

For some reason that made Sunset feel better. And beside him Gail was nodding as well.

"Someone mounted the crystal on a necklace?" Patty asked.

"Harmonia did that," Ben said. "Or Harmony as I guess she is called in this time. From that point forward it became known as the Necklace Stone. She kept the necklace close to make sure it wouldn't fall into the wrong hands. But it was supposedly lost in the fall of Atlantis."

"You all were around during Atlantis?" Sunset asked. "Atlantis was a real thing?"

"Very real," Ben said, nodding.

"I'm not that old by a long ways," Poker Boy said, shaking his head.

"Neither am I," Patty said.

"We were both there," Ben said, indicating himself and Stan who had been sitting quietly, sipping on a chocolate milkshake. "Laverne and Dottie were both there as well."

"Wow," Gail said softly.

Sunset felt the same way exactly. He felt like he had been around a long time being a Ghost Agent for a hundred years, but compared to these folks, he was a baby. He could only imagine how Gail was feeling right now. They would have to talk about it later.

"So there is bad blood between Dottie and Harmony?" Poker Boy asked.

Ben nodded. "They were married for almost a thousand years. A complete love match in their time."

"Oh," Patty said.

"Didn't end well I take it?" Poker Boy asked.

Sunset was starting to really like Poker Boy. He just said what he was thinking. Sunset sometimes wished he could do that.

"They got separated during the destruction of Atlantis," Ben said. "Dottie never stopped looking for her and by the time Dottie discovered Harmony was still alive, five hundred years had passed and Harmony was married to Cadmus and living in Greece. They had a pack of kids as well."

"Let me guess," Poker Boy said, "They haven't spoken since."

Ben just sort of nodded and said nothing.

"How many years are we talking about?" Sunset asked.

"Five thousand or so," Ben said. "Give or take a few centuries."

Sunset couldn't believe how silly this entire case had become. And deadly serious at the same time.

"So," Gail said, "Our best bet on tracking this brain-washing program and the person or people behind it is Dottie. And Dottie won't even try it unless she has the protection of a Necklace Stone from her ex-spouse whom she hasn't talked to in centuries. And the stone might be lost anyway. Do I have that right?"

Jewel nodded. "I'm reading that the same way.

"Sounds to me like a typical day around here," Poker Boy said, munching on a fry. "I'm up for helping if you want me?"

"Please," Sunset said. Gail, Jewel, and Tommy nodded.

"Call me if you need help," Stan said and vanished.

"I think I should go with you as well," Ben said. "Harmony was a good friend of mine."

"That would help," Sunset said.

"Sorry I can't join the fun," Patty said, "but work calls."

She kissed Poker Boy on the cheek and also vanished.

So now they were down to six.

Jewel glanced at Sunset and Gail. "I think Tommy and I should fade back on this one as well. Too many ghosts might overwhelm the poor woman."

"I'll call you when we get some answers," Gail said.

Jewel and Tommy vanished and then they were four.

Sunset just had to smile. His partners were a brand new ghost, a famous superhero, and an old god. That was too stupid for even a television sitcom.

Sixteen

ail and Sunset jumped with Poker Boy and the older Ben to a small room that smelled faintly of unwashed gym socks. The place was clearly a waiting room with a dozen chairs and two windows, one that looked out at an empty school hallway and the other that looked out over a street lined with parked cars.

The floor was scuffed tile and a wooden desk sat on one side facing the chairs. The desk didn't look used at all.

The sound of kids laughing and talking came from outside the windows of the room in the hallway.

Gail didn't know how she felt other than numb. This was all happening so fast. In five months she had barely gotten used to the fact that she was a ghost and could help people, now she was learning that gods really did exist and some of them had been around for a very, very long time.

And they just worked regular jobs. Clearly both Patty and

Dottie worked. Gail couldn't quite grasp that the god of computers worked as a clerk at an Apple store.

Gail hadn't gotten a chance to ask Sunset who the thin, powerful woman was who had appeared first in Poker Boy's diner-slash-office. Clearly she was someone very powerful and used to being in control of things. But Gail had never heard of a god named Laverne before.

But Gail had heard of Harmonia, a Greek goddess who seemed to now be going by the name of Harmony and working at a local high school in Las Vegas. All this was going to take some getting used to.

Ben moved over to a closed inner door in the small waiting room and knocked.

A woman's voice on the other side said, "Come in."

Ben glanced at the rest of them and opened the door, moving into the small office beyond.

The woman sitting at the large wooden desk looked to be no more than thirty, with short blonde hair and green eyes. She glanced up with a smile as if greeting a student.

The office felt comfortable, with shelves of books behind the desk and two chairs in front. A large window had the blinds open allowing the morning sun to shine in.

It took a moment, then the woman beamed and said, "Ben!"

She jumped up and moved around the desk and hugged Ben and he hugged her back.

Harmony was wearing dress slacks and a cloth blouse and tennis shoes. Gail liked how Harmony dressed for her job. Comfortable, yet business.

"Been far too long," she said, smiling at Ben.

"It has been," Ben said. "And that's on me."

"I heard you moved over from the lamplighters to library work," she said. "A perfect fit for you."

"It is," Ben said. "And I want you to meet the person responsible for saving me from fading away to nothingness. This is Poker Boy."

Again, Harmony beamed as she shook Poker Boy's hand. "I have heard some wonderful things about you and your team. Everyone owes you more than just thank you for saving the world so many times."

"Appreciate that," Poker Boy said, smiling in return. "We couldn't do much of what we do without Ben helping us, though."

"And that's no surprise," Harmony said.

Ben just smiled and shook his head. Then he turned to Sunset and Gail. "Harmony, I'd like you to meet two of the Ghost of a Chance agents. This is Sunset and this is Gail."

Harmony looked puzzled. "Who?"

Gail glanced at Sunset. Clearly Harmony couldn't see them.

"Oh, sorry," Ben said. "Forgot. Laverne, a little help."

A moment later Harmony stepped back as clearly she could suddenly see the two Ghost Agents.

"Well, that was strange," Harmony said, smiling. "Until this moment I didn't know the Ghost of a Chance agents were anything more than a myth."

"We've worked with the agents a number of times," Poker Boy said. "They are great."

"Well, happy meeting you as well," Harmony said. "Do all Ghost Agents dress so well?"

Sunset laughed and said, "Just habits from when we were alive."

Harmony nodded and turned and moved around behind her desk, indicating that Ben and Poker Boy should sit in the two chairs.

"So I assume the four of you are here for a reason," Harmony said, settling back in her chair as if ready to listen to a student.

Gail stood beside Sunset and watched and listened as Ben and Poker Boy explained the problem of the brainwashing program and what they were trying to do."

"Let me guess," Harmony said, "You want Dottie to track the program back to the controller."

Ben nodded. "She said she didn't really want to attempt it without some protection."

Harmony nodded, sitting back and thinking. "The Necklace Stone."

Ben simply said, "Yes. Does it still exist?"

"It does," Harmony said.

Gail couldn't even begin to imagine what Harmony was thinking. Or if the bad blood with Dottie still existed after so many centuries on Harmony's side. There was clearly still some bitterness on Dottie's side.

"That program as dangerous as it seems?" Harmony asked.

"We think so," Sunset said.

Gail nodded. "We believe the company they took over

could very well be a test run of some sort. Something much larger."

"That kind of power would make sense that it would be tested like that," Harmony said. "And no computer program can do that."

Gail and Ben both nodded to that. Gail had no doubt that something outside of programming was going on and clearly so did Dottie and now Harmony when they heard about it.

"The technology that could do that was owned by the Atlantis Head Council," Harmony said. "It was called the Mind Stone. It was only used on the worst criminals of the time. How did you all free the employees from the affects of the Mind Stone?"

Gail wasn't surprised that it had a name. She and Sunset explained how they could go inside of live people and had just erased the memory of the brainwashing."

"Wow, Ghost Agents can do that?" Harmony said, nodding. "No wonder you are teaming with them, Poker Boy."

He laughed. "Just learned that tidbit about erasing parts myself this morning."

"A good skill to have," Harmony said. "Especially handy in counseling in trauma cases."

"Used it a few times for exactly that," Sunset said, nodding. "I'll be glad to volunteer if you ever need my help on something. Or to just get to the bottom of a problem in a person's mind."

"I will be glad to help as well," Gail said.

"Thank you," Harmony said. "I really do appreciate that and more than likely will ask for that kind of help at times."

She sat thinking for a moment, then she looked at Ben. "Dottie thinks she can trace this attacker?"

"She does," Ben said, nodding.

"And she's right that she would need the Necklace Stone if she came face-to-face with someone wielding the Mind Stone against her."

Ben nodded.

Gail just sat and watched.

After a moment Harmony nodded. "I'll go with her, but we will need you two Ghost Agents to go along as well. We might need you to control who we find on the other side. And Poker Boy, you and one of your team should also go. The necklace, through me, can protect us all."

Ben and Poker Boy both nodded.

"Tell Dottie it will be good to see her again," Harmony said. "I'll be off in two hours. We need to get this done before anything worse happens with that Mind Stone."

"Thanks," Ben said. "We'll be in Poker Boy's office when you are ready."

"Yes, thank you," Gail said as Poker Boy and Ben stood.

A moment later they were back in Poker Boy's office.

A second later the woman named Laverne appeared. "She agreed?"

"She did," Ben said. "Two hours and we'll jump from here. You want to tell Dottie or you want me to."

Laverne smiled. "I'll tell her. This could be fun. Get a fast laptop hooked up here to the Internet. Dottie's going to need that."

Laverne vanished and Poker Boy sat down in the booth laughing.

Gail looked around at the fantastic view of Las Vegas and the mountains around the valley. What in the world were they facing?

In the next two hours, she really needed some answers to that question.

Seventeen

S unset sat with Gail and Ben and Poker Boy in the huge booth in the floating office above Las Vegas. They sat where Stan the God of Poker had been sitting earlier, leaving the end of the booth open. This was not at all how he had imagined his day was going go. Especially after the wonderful start of waking up next to Gail.

In front of them were two wonderful cheeseburgers and a basket of fries and a milkshake. And spread out around them the fantastic view of Las Vegas on a clear, sunny day.

Both Poker Boy and Ben were stunned as they watched Sunset and Gail eat. Poker Boy and Ben could see the Ghost Agents eat, yet the main food never moved from its spot on the table.

"Does that taste thinner?" Poker Boy asked as Sunset took a bite of the ghost part of the cheeseburger, leaving the real cheeseburger sitting on the plate untouched.

"Actually a thousand times better," Gail said before he could answer. "It's like we are eating the very essence, the pure flavor of food."

"Everything is better as a ghost," Sunset said. He smiled at Gail and she blushed. He loved that.

As the next hour went by, he and Gail and Poker Boy asked questions of Ben about the Mind Stone and the Necklace Stone that was supposed to protect them from being brainwashed.

"Both were far-advanced tech," Ben said. "The Mind Stone was used in the war with the Titans and helped turn the outcome of the battle. The stone on the necklace was used by those wielding the Mind Stone to protect themselves from its powers."

Poker Boy looked startled. "So the person using the Mind Stone might have a stone similar to what is on Harmony's necklace?"

"Yes," Ben said, nodding.

Sunset didn't like the sound of that at all.

"Is the person or persons on the other side going to be able to see me and Sunset?" Gail asked.

"More than likely not," Ben said. "The only reason we can see you is that Laverne gave us the power to be able to do that."

"So who exactly is Laverne?" Gail asked.

Poker Boy laughed.

Sunset just put his hand on her leg and smiled. Gail was going to have a very hard time with this one.

"Laverne," Sunset said, "is Lady Luck."

"She pretty much runs everything," Poker Boy said.

Gail looked first at Poker Boy, then at Sunset, clearly wanting to say something, but then changing her mind.

Sunset leaned over and kissed her on the cheek. "Being a ghost is never dull, is it?"

She just laughed and said, "Never."

At that moment Laverne and Dottie appeared. And as they did Madge, the waitress in the far-too-tight fifties diner uniform came out of a back door to the office carrying a laptop computer.

Laverne and Dottie pulled up chairs to the booth table and sat down.

Dottie opened the laptop and got it going, then turned to Sunset. "When we are ready, I'm going to need you to be in my head to show me exactly what you saw in that office and the computer connection you tried to trace."

Sunset nodded. He couldn't imagine being inside a god's head, but he would do what he could do.

Dottie laughed at Sunset. "Don't worry kid, I won't let you see anything you're not supposed to see in there."

"Appreciate that," Sunset said, smiling at her.

Dottie turned to Gail. "You are going to need to be riding along inside Harmony's mind, showing her the same thing. Can the two of you be linked up while in two different people's minds?"

"If you and Harmony are holding hands," Sunset said. "That way Gail and I can know what both of you are doing at the same time."

"And we can keep the two of you connected as well," Gail said.

Dottie frowned, but said nothing, instead focusing on the computer in front of her.

Laverne just smiled and Poker Boy managed to keep a complete poker face.

Sunset had no doubt what they were about to do was going to be interesting, to say the least.

Eighteen

Tense didn't begin to describe the moment when Harmony arrived. At first she did what Gail guessed most visitors to this office did the first time. Harmony gasped and looked around.

Then she turned and saw Dottie and Harmony's face turned white.

Dottie glanced up from the computer and over her shoulder. "Hi, H. How you been?"

Then Dottie turned back to what she was doing on the computer.

Gail watched as Harmony took a deep breath and came toward the table. She sat down on the other side of Laverne.

Silence filled the office, a tense, uneasy silence until finally Dottie said, "Sunset. Need you to give me what you saw on those computers in that office."

Sunset nodded, glanced at Gail and then moved over and vanished into Dottie.

"Okay," Poker Boy said, shaking his head. "No matter how often I watch that it doesn't get any less creepy."

Gail watched as Dottie nodded and her fingers seemed to become a blur on the keyboard.

Then Dottie said, "Gail, need you in H. Poker Boy, you and Ben ready to go?"

Laverne stood and stepped back and Harmony moved over beside Dottie.

"Ready?" Gail asked.

Harmony nodded and Gail moved over and went inside her.

Harmony had most of her brain walled off. Gail found a spot that felt like she was standing off to one side of Harmony's mind and then said simply, "I'm here."

"Understood," Harmony said out loud.

"Put your hand on my shoulder and don't let go," Dottie said to Harmony.

Harmony did and Gail was almost overwhelmed by the emotion of love and missing Dottie that Harmony felt before she could get it under control.

Sunset said, "You here, Gail?"

Gail imagined herself moving up into Harmony's shoulder and reaching across to hold Sunset's hand.

"We're ready," Sunset said to Dottie.

Harmony extended the screen around them from the stone on the necklace she was wearing.

"We're ready as well," Gail said.

Poker Boy and Ben had moved out of the booth and were touching Dottie and Harmony's shoulders.

"Here we go," Dottie said. "Laverne, track us as much as you can."

With that Gail felt Dottie jump them.

They ended up standing in a large, ornate, oak-shelved office. A massive number of books filled the walls and a gigantic oak desk filled one side of the room, empty.

The ceiling had to be twenty feet overhead and looked to be inlaid in some sort of gold.

Decorative rugs in gold and browns covered the floor under couches and a few chairs all faced the desk.

Gail had never seen a room like it.

There was no one in the room and no sign at all of computers.

"Jump us back!" Harmony shouted. "Now!"

The panic in Harmony's mind was almost too much for Gail to handle and she put up screens against the waves of emotion.

Sunset was having the same problem with panic coming from Dottie.

"I can't," Dottie said. "My computer didn't come with me."

"Wouldn't work here anyway," Harmony said.

"Someone want to explain where we are?" Poker Boy asked as Ben moved over and dropped down onto a chair. He looked completely defeated.

Outside the room sirens were wailing.

Gail read from Harmony's mind that those were warning sirens, telling everyone to take cover.

Then Gail realized what Harmony was thinking.

She stepped out of Harmony at the same instant that Sunset stepped out of Dottie.

"What happened?" Poker Boy asked. "Where are we?"

Gail reached over and held onto Sunset's hand.

Harmony kept her hand on Dottie's shoulder.

"Not so much as to where we are," Ben said from the chair he had sat down in. "It's when."

"When?" Poker Boy asked.

Gail knew the answer because both Harmony and Dottie had recognized the room instantly.

"This is the High Chancellor of Atlantis's office," Ben said. "And those sirens mean Atlantis is breaking apart as we stand here."

"That can't be possible," Poker Boy said.

But Gail knew it was.

And she knew the history that Harmony and Dottie had had in this office.

"What have we done?" Harmony said.

"It seems we are about to repeat our own past," Dottie said.

Harmony nodded.

She took her hand away from Dottie and looked directly at Poker Boy and Ben. "The four of us need to hide. Gail, Ben, you two stay and watch what happens next for us."

"Why?" Poker Boy asked.

"Because if this really is what it seems to be," Harmony said, "Dottie and I are about to rob this place."

Dottie laughed. "Interesting we came back to the scene of the crime, isn't it?"

"Very," Harmony said. "Back to the beginning of our end."

Nineteen

Sunset knew that something wasn't right the moment both Dottie and Harmony got upset.

Somehow, they believed that they were back at the end of Atlantis. But that couldn't be possible any more than the employees of that scam investment firm thought they were selling good investments.

As the four live people scrambled for a door out the back of the large room, Sunset turned to Gail who was looking shocked and a little panicked.

"We're not really here," Sunset said. "We're being duped just as those people in that firm were duped."

"Are you sure?" Gail said, indicating the room around them. "This sure feels real."

"It sure does," Sunset said. "Would you let me into your mind, see if I can find the spot where we were brainwashed?"

"Please," Gail said. "Anything to make this end."

Sunset took her hand and a moment later he was in her mind, something he hadn't ever done with another Ghost Agent before.

He could instantly see how much she cared about him, which made him happy.

"Hurry, someone's coming," Gail said.

Through her he could hear the door starting to open.

He focused on the last few seconds right before they jumped away from Poker Boy's office and made the entire thing slow down, like watching everything in slow motion.

And the moment he did that, he saw the issue. They had never really jumped anywhere.

He carefully took that moment around that jump point in Gail's mind and blocked it off and shrank it down.

"What?" she asked, suddenly back inside of Harmony.

Sunset quickly showed her what he had done and had her do the same for him, cutting out the mind control that made him think they had jumped back in time.

Then they carefully, at the same time, did the same for Dottie and Harmony.

Then they left their minds, stepping back into Poker Boy's office.

"What happened?" Laverne said. "None of you jumped."

Dottie slammed the lid on the computer closed and stood up. "Whoever is behind this got us before we could even move. The moment I linked into the origin site."

"The stone didn't protect us," Harmony said softly.

"It did," Dottie said. "Just not in the right way at the right moment. We were not ready for that kind of attack."

"Thank you," Harmony said turning to Sunset and Gail. "I assume you saved us by cutting out the brain control moment."

"We did," Sunset said.

"That damned office was like returning to a nightmare," Dottie said.

"What office?" Laverne asked.

"The Atlantis Chancellor's office right before the moment of destruction," Dottie said.

"Oh," Laverne said.

"I think Sunset and I need to clear Ben and Poker Boy," Gail said.

Laverne laughed as the five of them looked at the frozen faces of Poker Boy and Ben still standing where they had been before the jump.

"You take Ben," Sunset said to Gail. "I'll get Poker Boy back."

Gail nodded.

A moment later he had the brainwashing moment out of Poker Boy's mind and stepped away.

"Damn am I glad that wasn't real," Poker Boy said.

Ben only nodded. "Not a place I ever wanted to return to."

Sunset looked at Dottie and Harmony and Ben. That was it. Sunset now knew how they could figure out who was behind this.

"Who would know that room would torture all three of you?" Ben asked.

Gail nodded. "Or that it even existed?"

"And have enough power to stage an instant attack the moment you linked up?" Sunset asked.

Dottie and Laverne and Ben all looked blank, but Harmony shook her head, then said, "Damn him all to hell."

And with that she turned and moved over to the edge of the room and stared out at the city below.

"Damn who?" Laverne asked.

Harmony shook her head slowly, keeping her back to all of them.

Dottie moved over to Harmony and put a hand gently on her shoulder. "Who could do this?"

"That bastard ex-husband of mine," Harmony said. "The one who brainwashed me into marrying him instead of continuing to look for you."

"He did what?" Dottie asked.

"Cadmus?" Laverne said, her voice low and mean.

Harmony nodded. "He told me the Mind Stone that went along with the Necklace Stone was destroyed, but I always half believed he had it and had used it on me."

Then Harmony spun around and looked at Sunset and Gail. "Could you two dig out an ancient brainwashing if it really did happen?"

Sunset looked at Gail, then turned back to Harmony. "If you wouldn't mind opening up to us, we could try."

"You were brain controlled by Cadmus?" Dottie asked, her voice soft.

"Let's find the hell out, shall we?" Harmony said.

She moved over and sat down in a chair facing the booth.

Sunset just looked at Gail, who was looking as worried as he was feeling.

They were going to dig back through the memories of thousands of years of a god.

What could possibly go wrong?

Twenty

The tension in Poker Boy's floating office felt so heavy, it was amazing the thing stayed in the air.

Gail took a deep breath and smiled at Sunset, who was looking as concerned as she was feeling.

"Harmony," Gail said. "Can you focus on the time and place you think you changed?"

Harmony nodded. "Haven't wanted to think about it for centuries, but I can do that."

Gail took Sunset's hand.

"We'll see what we can find," Sunset said.

Then the two of them stepped inside Harmony.

Gail was stunned at the anger Harmony was feeling. And the emotions she blocked out trying to focus on the time.

"We find where she was still looking for Dottie," Sunset said. "Then moved forward in time from there."

"Right here," Gail said, seeing clearly the intensity of

Harmony's search. The world at that point was in ruins with pockets of the old civilization that had been Atlantis fading back into the dark ages.

Gail moved them forward through time in Harmony's mind like fast-forwarding through a movie until Harmony met Cadmus. He seemed handsome, kind, and wanted to help. He had built a city and a large compound on a hillside and had all the modern things she loved about Atlantis protected and still in use.

But Harmony knew she couldn't stay there long. She had to keep searching.

Sunset moved them forward a few more days and Harmony had decided to stay with Cadmus.

"In those two days," Gail said.

"Agreed," Sunset said.

Gail moved them back in time in Harmony's memories, again like a movie running quickly in reverse, images just flashing past, and then forward until a dinner with Cadmus on the night before Harmony planned on leaving.

And there it was. Clear as day.

He had altered her mind to forget her quest and stay with him.

What a bastard.

Cadmus had basically raped Harmony's mind.

Now Gail felt angry and she could tell that Sunset was as well.

"You stay here at this spot in the memory," Gail said. "I'm going to step out and ask Harmony exactly what she wants us to do."

Sunset let go of her hand and Gail stepped out of Harmony and back into the light of Poker Boy's office.

If she thought the tension was thick before they went into Harmony's mind, now it was suffocating.

Harmony and Dottie both looked at Gail like she was about to tell them they were going to die.

"The night you were having a last dinner with Cadmus," Gail said to Harmony, "before going back on your search for Dottie, Cadmus brainwashed you with the Mind Stone. We have the exact moment and time."

"I will kill that bastard," Harmony said, her voice low and mean.

"I will help you," Dottie said.

"What would you like us to do?" Gail asked. "Blocking off that brainwashing moment now will not change the history, but it might change how you view the memories of him and your five children with him."

"He held me prisoner against my will," Harmony said. "Cut that moment out and I will live with the rest. Clear the brainwashing."

Gail nodded and stepped back into Harmony and beside Sunset.

"I got this," Sunset said, taking Gail's hand.

A white bubble formed around the entire moment when Cadmus used the stone to brainwash Harmony. And Sunset then tightened the bubble down harder and harder until that entire moment of brainwashing was now gone from Harmony's mind.

Then they stepped out of Harmony.

She was blinking, as if just waking up from a long nap.

Then she slowly turned to Dottie as tears started to run down Harmony's face.

"I am so, so sorry," Harmony said, sobbing.

With that the two ancient gods were in each other's arms crying.

Love derailed thousands of years before now clearly still existed.

How wonderful was that?

PART FOUR

A God Fight

Twenty-One

Sunset watched Harmony and Dottie hug and cry for a moment, then started watching Laverne, the most powerful god of them all.

In the floating office the tension was thick. Very, very thick. Almost to the point the air felt heavy and hard to breathe.

Clearly Laverne was not happy.

In fact, Lady Luck was radiating anger.

Sunset bet that passengers on the planes coming into the Las Vegas airport could feel it and more than likely fights were breaking out in the casinos below.

It was that powerful of an anger.

Poker Boy and Ben sat in the booth and tried to pretend they were not there.

Finally Harmony turned to Sunset and Gail. "Thank you for freeing me."

"You are more than welcome," Gail said.

Sunset just let himself nod and bow slightly.

"So now we have a major problem to deal with named Cadmus," Laverne said.

Sunset almost shivered because Laverne's words were so cold and angry.

Making Lady Luck angry was never, ever a good plan.

"Do you know where Cadmus is?" Dottie asked.

"No," Laverne said. "He is blocking me."

"He has a compound in the hills of Greece," Harmony said. "He was always trying to get me to talk with him and come back and live with him."

"That compound can't be breached in any conventional way," Laverne said, nodding. "I know of the place. I would not doubt he has a small army inside it and let's not forget his powers without the Mind Stone."

"What are his powers?" Poker Boy asked.

"Too much for most of us," Dottie said and Poker Boy just nodded.

Sunset glanced at Gail who nodded. They were clearly thinking along the same lines.

"Let the Ghost Agents go in," Sunset said.

"Will he be able to see us?" Gail asked.

"No," Laverne said. "I am the only one who knows how to make a Ghost Agent visible to a god or superhero."

"Will he sense them?" Poker Boy asked. "We did this once before but the god could sense the Ghost Agents."

Sunset would have to ask Poker Boy about that when he had a chance.

"We can attack him at the same time and keep him busy if he can sense you," Dottie said, pointing at the computer.

"He's so arrogant that I doubt he would consider anyone actually coming at him from inside his compound," Harmony said.

Dottie and Laverne both nodded to that.

Sunset turned to Ben. "Would you be able to get exact plans and location of his compound for us?"

Ben nodded. "It will be in the records. I will get them now."

He vanished.

"So what will you be able to do to him?" Poker Boy asked.

"If we can get inside his body," Sunset said, smiling. "Just about anything."

"Oh," Poker Boy said, not breaking his poker face.

"We will need Jewel and Tommy on this as well," Gail said.

Laverne turned to Harmony. "You know him better than anyone. Could this work?"

"If he was distracted, yes," Harmony said.

Laverne took a deep breath. "All right. We have two missions here. One is to get the Mind Stone from him and get it to safety in my office."

Sunset nodded as everyone else did. After seeing what that Mind Stone could do to an entire office of people as well as Harmony, he wanted it out of commission completely.

"Second, we capture Cadmus. Let me deal with him under the rules."

Sunset swore that when Lady Luck said the words 'the rules' the entire floating office shook.

Poker Boy actually looked like his face went white with that.

Dottie and Harmony both just nodded.

"We would like a say in Cadmus's fate," Harmony said, touching Dottie.

"And you will have it," Laverne said.

She turned to Poker Boy and Sunset and Gail. "You three along with Jewel and Tommy develop a plan with Ben when he gets back. I want to be ready to move on this in two hours."

All three of them nodded like their heads were being pulled by the same string. Sunset had never had a direct order from Lady Luck before. It carried the weight of a train hitting you.

"You two come with me," Laverne said to Dottie and Harmony. "We have some history to discuss."

With that, the three gods vanished.

"Well, this is going to be interesting," Poker Boy said, shaking his head.

Sunset could only nod to that massive understatement.

Twenty-Two

Gail watched as Madge put some fresh fries and milkshakes on the table in front of all of them. The fries smelled wonderful and looked like they were perfectly salted.

Madge also put some glasses of water on the table and Gail went for one of those first. Something about roaming around in a god's mind in ancient pre-history had made her thirsty. Or maybe it was because she felt so far, far out of her depth here it wasn't even funny.

Less than a year ago she had been a happy prosecuting attorney on the Oregon Coast, trying to make her little coastal towns safer. Dealing with gods and ghosts and super-heroes sure never would have crossed her mind. Not even in a fever dream.

Jewel and Tommy had returned and Ben had returned with the plans of the Cadmus compound.

Around the large booth in the floating office in the sky were Poker Boy, Ben, Jewel and Tommy, and Sunset and her. And there was enough room in the booth for a couple more, the booth was so big.

Jewel and Tommy told them about the last time they had tried this with another god named Numa inside of another compound. It seemed that gods liked compounds or something.

Gail didn't like the part of the story where the god had trapped the Ghost Agents in his own body. So Jewel and Tommy had a plan this time to avoid that, which Gail was very happy to hear.

It seemed that they had taken on Numa and now were using his entire compound as a headquarters for Ghost Agents. Plus it had made all of the Ghost Agents very rich. Jewel and Tommy had said nothing about that, and since Sunset had already made himself rich in real world money, it had never occurred to Gail to ask.

After this mission, she would.

When Sunset heard about all the other agents, he asked if it might not be a good idea to bring them in as well. Jewel shook her head.

"We would have to get them up to speed on the Mind Stone and besides," Jewel said, "I would rather have them as backup."

Gail liked the sound of that a lot, actually.

By the time the two hours were up, they had a plan. Only Sunset would go into Cadmus's body first. Jewel and Tommy would be inside household staff and military, getting them close to Cadmus and getting ready to make them stand down and leave the compound. But not until Cadmus was out of the picture.

Gail would stay with Dottie and Harmony on the direct attack.

"More than likely," Poker Boy said, "Cadmus has all his people under some sort of Mind Stone control. You are going to need to break that before they will do anything."

"Like we did in the office building," Tommy said.

"We can do that," Sunset said, nodding.

Gail just hoped they could. Dealing with brainwashed office workers was one thing, going against the military and staff of a god might be another level of brainwashing.

"We're going to have to walk in," Jewel said, looking at the plans of the massive compound.

Tommy nodded. "More than likely his protective screens will be up around the complex, only allowing certain people through. The three of us will have to be nothing more than a dot in one of those people moving inside. It was us transporting through a screen and also getting Numa's people to stand down before we got to Numa that alerted him to our presence."

Gail nodded to that.

Thankfully, Tommy and Jewel had some experience with this. Gail had a hunch this was going to be very different, but at least it felt like they knew what they were doing going in.

Gail really wanted to ask if ghosts could die. It had not once come up in the training, but it was clear that ghosts could be trapped from what happened the last time Jewel and

Tommy tried this. And being trapped for eternity scared Gail a lot more than dying again.

She decided to hold off that death question until after this was all over. No point in scaring herself anymore than she already was.

At that moment Laverne and Dottie and Harmony appeared. All three of them took chairs at the end of the large booth and Dottie put her laptop on top of the table, but didn't open it.

All three of them were determined.

"We are fairly certain that Cadmus does not know Harmony and Dottie and Ben and Poker Boy escaped that last trap," Laverne said.

"So I'm going to ride us in over the top of what he did last time to us," Dottie said. "When you are all in position."

Laverne looked at the four Ghost Agents. "Are you ready?"

"We are," Jewel said.

Gail managed to nod.

"We have a set timeline worked out," Poker Boy said. "At exactly one hour, you start the computer attack. Ben and I will ride with you on that."

Laverne nodded.

"We will need one of you to stay with us," Dottie said to the four Ghost Agents.

"I will be doing that," Gail said. "Sunset and I have a connection so I will know if they are in trouble. And I can help you in case the Mind Stone traps you again."

"Get the shields down on that compound," Laverne said

to Tommy and Jewel and Sunset. "The moment that happens I will deal with Cadmus."

Gail managed to not shudder. Lady Luck really had a way with radiating power.

And right now she was pissed.

Wow.

Twenty-Three

Sunset and Tommy and Jewel jumped to a spot just outside of Cadmus's main compound gate.

Sunset was surprised. The air was hot and very dry and the light felt even more intense and bright than it had in Las Vegas. Around them were rocky hills covered in some sort of blue-green tree and brush. In front of the three of them was an ancient stone wall with a gate.

But nothing ancient about the men standing with guns in guard stations on the walls.

The walls wound over the hills in both directions and the main compound inside could not be seen from this point.

A truck was parked at the gate and the driver and a guard were talking, checking papers. Then two of the guards checked the cargo of the truck. From what Sunset could tell it was fruits and other food items.

"The driver," Tommy said.

They moved quickly to him and climbed up into the cab and vanished inside him. Then all three of them made themselves as small as they could, tucked back in the man's head so that they could see through him where they were going, but with luck not be noticed.

The guy's name was Meletios and he had a wife, three kids, and a thriving delivery business. He delivered to this compound twice every day and always had to go through the same process, which he found annoying and stupid.

Sunset and Tommy and Jewel watched for any signs that their presence had been spotted as Meletios drove his truck in and over a slight ridge on the two-lane paved road, heading toward a large compound tucked against one hill.

The compound was huge and clearly opulent. Meletios thought it was gaudy and stupid and a waste of wealth.

The main home in the back and on the highest point had the kitchen he was delivering his cargo to. On the left were large stone buildings that housed hundreds of soldiers and on the right large modern office buildings Meletios had never been allowed to go near.

Those buildings worried Sunset and he whispered that to Tommy and Jewel and they both nodded.

Why this god would take the time and energy to brainwash an investment firm in Portland, Oregon, was making less and less sense. There was a lot going on here they hadn't discovered yet.

Meletios pulled his truck up to the service entrance to the main building and went inside with his inventory clipboard to get help unloading.

At that moment, once inside the service area, inside the walls of the building, Sunset and Tommy and Jewel stepped out of their ride.

They moved past the modern kitchen area that looked like it could have been right out of any restaurant in Las Vegas and into the main part of the house.

The corridor had high ceilings with thick wood beams spaced along them. Some sort of stucco walls were decorated with tapestries and art of all colors and the floors were polished stone.

The place felt and looked like a palace.

A man who looked like a house cleaner came past and Tommy motioned for Sunset and Jewel to stay put and he slid inside the man. A moment later Tommy came out.

"This way," he said.

Sunset followed Tommy and Jewel, moving quickly through the wide corridor.

Until they found one large wooden door.

"Cadmus has a suite behind this door," Tommy said.

At that moment two men in New York style business suits came from the other direction down the hallway and started to go through the door.

"Good luck," Tommy said as Sunset went into one and Jewel into the other.

Sunset was instantly stunned at who he was riding inside. The man's name was Loman Foley and he was head of an investment bank out of Las Angeles. The man Jewel was in was his partner.

The buildings on the grounds were investment companies. And they were moving billions, slowly taking over more and more of the world's resources.

The small investment firm in Portland was only a tiny tip of a massive iceberg.

Sunset went into the man's history and found where the Mind Stone had brainwashed the man.

Sunset put a field around the entire thing and the memory of the last three years, but did nothing.

The two men knocked on Cadmus's office door and someone on the other side they recognized as Cadmus said, "Enter."

Sunset knew that Loman and his partner were there to give Cadmus his daily briefing on the progress they were making.

"Now!" Sunset said through the connection he had with Gail back in Poker Boy's office.

Gail said simply, "Moving."

As the two men stopped in front of Cadmus, Sunset was shocked at what the ancient god looked like. He had been expecting some sort of Zeus figure, but instead Cadmus looked to be no more than forty and blonde, with a chiseled chin and bright green eyes. He had on a silk dress shirt and no tie.

Just as with Laverne, the man radiated power.

He sat behind a massive wooden desk with computers on it. The walls were filled with what looked to be ancient books and on one wall a large stone fireplace was in front of a group of chairs and a dark couch.

The two men in suits stopped in front of Cadmus's large

desk and Cadmus sat back in his large office chair, ready to listen.

As Lowman was about to start his report, Cadmus suddenly leaned forward toward his computer.

"That is not possible."

Clearly Cadmus had gotten an alarm about Dottie's attack.

At that moment Sunset shrunk the bubble around Lowman's brainwashing and gave him the instruction to just stand still until otherwise ordered.

Then Sunset stepped out of Lowman just as Tommy vanished inside of Cadmus.

Beside Sunset, Jewel appeared and instantly went with Tommy inside of Cadmus.

All Sunset could do was be their backup in case something went wrong.

The ancient god had his fingers poised on the computer screen when suddenly he tipped over to his side and rolled out of his chair. His head cracked the stone floor, which was going to hurt if he ever woke up.

He lay sprawled on the stone on his back, legs apart. His eyes were open and staring at the ceiling.

An instant later Laverne appeared in the room alongside Dottie and Harmony.

Dottie had her arm around Harmony who looked like she was going to be sick when she saw the ancient god on the floor.

Gail was with them and Sunset couldn't remember being

so happy to see someone in a long time. And they had only been apart for an hour.

Gail hugged him and he hugged her back.

"Glad you are safe," Gail said.

Tommy and Jewel appeared from Cadmus, smiling.

The two men looked at Laverne with puzzled looks on their faces.

"They remember nothing about the last five years," Jewel said. "We left commands that they are to do as told."

Laverne nodded. "Please go home to your families and say nothing about this to anyone. Understood?"

Both men nodded and just about ran from the room.

Sunset tried not to smile at that.

"What did you do to him?" Laverne asked, indicating Cadmus.

Jewel smiled. "We shrunk his entire mind down inside of a small ball and disconnected control from his entire body. "He will continue to live fine, but he has no control of anything."

"Can you bring his mind back?" Laverne asked.

"At any point," Tommy said. "He is still in there and can hear everything that is being said by you right now. And his mind can feel the pain and everything his body needs, but he cannot control or react."

"But he feels the pain?" Dottie asked.

"He does," Tommy said. "He has a bad headache from hitting his head on the stone. And right now I bet he is getting very, very angry."

"You put his mind in jail, basically," Harmony said.

"Yes," Jewel said.

"There is no way he can get out of that jail, either," Tommy said. "But he will still need to be watched and one of us will need to check on him at times."

Laverne nodded.

Sunset liked the sound of that.

Harmony walked over to Cadmus and bent down and opened up his shirt. On a chain under his shirt was a pendant. She yanked it off, not caring that it ripped skin.

Sunset figured that was the Mind Stone.

Then Harmony stood and took off the pendant she wore and handed both to Laverne.

Laverne looked at both and nodded, then put Cadmus's Mind Stone in her pocket and handed the other one back to Harmony.

Sunset watched as Harmony nodded thanks, then put her pendant back around her neck. At some point Sunset was going to need to ask why Laverne had done that.

Then Harmony bent over Cadmus again.

"You imprisoned me for centuries," she said, her voice mean and level. "You being imprisoned like this only suits your crime against me."

Harmony stood. "Under the rules, how long can you keep him like this?"

Laverne got an evil smile on her face. "He looks healthy to me. We will put him in a prison cell and feed him and take care of his needs. I am sure for a few centuries at least. That will be enough to follow the rules for his crimes not only against you, but for what he has done now. At least the crimes we know about now. If we discover more, the time might stretch."

"Thank you," Harmony said.

Then as Sunset watched, Harmony turned back to Cadmus. "And for all the pain you inflicted on me with that thing between your legs, expect me to visit you every few months to help in your healing."

With that she kicked him as hard as she could in the groin.

Sunset flinched, as did Tommy, but Cadmus just lay there, his eyes open, starting at the ceiling.

Wow, that had to hurt.

Then Harmony turned to Laverne, smiling. "I hope that helped his healing."

Laverne smiled and nodded. "I am sure it did. And I am sure he will look forward to his regular treatment."

Harmony laughed. "I know I will."

PART FIVE

Stopping the Unstoppable

Twenty-Four

Gail could not believe how worried she had been about Sunset. She was so much in love with him, it amazed her. She had never felt like that for anyone before.

And she liked it. Not the worry part, the love.

Right now, more than anything, she wanted them to be back in their wonderful condo in Portland celebrating the success they had just had. But she had a hunch they had a much, much larger problem now. She didn't know exactly what, but she could sense from Sunset the problem was immediate.

Just as Laverne and Harmony and Dottie were about to leave with Cadmus, Jewel stopped them.

"We have a very large problem to solve yet," Jewel said.

Gail watched as Sunset and Tommy both nodded.

Laverne looked puzzled.

"Those two office buildings here on the grounds are headquarters for a massive threat to civilization," Tommy said.

Gail almost gasped at that kind of language coming from Tommy. In her time training with them, neither he nor Jewel had been people who exaggerated.

Laverne actually raised one eyebrow at that.

"The two men who were here were major bankers, investment bankers," Sunset said, "and they both had been controlled by a Mind Stone.

"We cleared them," Jewel said, "but there are thousands in those two major buildings and maybe upwards of a million more around the world, many controlled by Mind Stone programming, all working to bring down the world economy by pulling massive amounts of money from it."

Gail actually felt sick to her stomach. The small scam they had discovered in Portland had only been a tiny tip of a massive problem.

"What can be done?" Laverne asked.

All three Ghost Agents shook their heads.

Laverne stared at them for a moment, then nodded. "Find out how far and wide this spreads," she said. "And how it is being spread. And where the money is going."

Gail nodded with Sunset and Tommy and Jewel.

Laverne turned to Dottie and Harmony. "I am going to need you both to be tracing through the computer world the Mind Stone programs and stopping them where you can."

Dottie and Harmony both nodded.

"I will get Poker Boy and his team working from their side

on this as well," Laverne said. "Everyone feed his team information as you have it. We meet in his office tomorrow at lunch to figure out what we can do to clean up Cadmus's mess."

Everyone nodded and with that the four gods left the four Ghost Agents standing in the massive, plush office.

Gail turned to look at Sunset. "Is it really that bad?"

Sunset nodded. "Worse."

Gail felt shocked. "How can it be worse?"

"We aren't sure yet," Jewel said, "but there might be more Mind Stones."

Gail thought she might be sick.

"It didn't feel like Cadmus was actually in control," Tommy said. "He thought he was, but it didn't feel like it."

"And I got that same sense from the man I was in," Sunset said, nodding. "But he didn't know who actually was."

"Oh," was all Gail could think to say.

This was a long way from over and that scared her more than she wanted to admit.

Twenty-Five

S unset kept his arm around Gail as the four of them stood in the lush office of Cadmus and planned their next move.

Jewel and Tommy decided that the four of them should stick together and not try to clear anyone, just find out any information they could. Sunset liked that idea and so did Gail.

"We need to see if there are more Mind Stones," Tommy said. "And who has them, without tipping our hand at any of this."

Sunset nodded.

So with that they jumped to the top floor of the tallest building inside Cadmus's compound.

The offices here were larger than Cadmus's office and very modern. Lush blue carpet covered the floors and a bank of computers filled the back wall of the largest office.

And one guy seemed to have that large office and be in control, at least here. He seemed to be in his forties, dressed in a silk suit, and a chiseled face and chin, like he had modeled when younger.

He radiated control, so they all four decided to climb inside him to get the same information before spreading out.

The guy's name was Kenyon and from what Sunset could tell the guy was president and CEO of about twenty different investment firms and banks around the world. And each investment firm ran or controlled hundreds of other corporations.

It was like a giant web of businesses with Kenyon sitting at the top of them all. And running it from this office.

He was rich beyond even his own imaginings. But that wasn't stopping him or even slowing him down.

Sunset slowly realized that Kenyon was only in charge of this branch. From what Sunset could tell, there were six other branches of banks, investment firms, and corporations as large.

Three women and four men ran the seven major businesses.

And they reported to a group of three, of which Cadmus had been one.

Kenyon hated Cadmus, thought him an idiot.

Their names of the other two were Rhesus and Sinon. Both lived together as a couple in the United States just outside of Las Vegas.

"Can anyone see the reason behind all of this?" Tommy asked.

"No," Gail said. "But Kenyon has been brainwashed."

"I see that," Jewel said.

"Can anyone see exactly what they are doing?"

"Everything I can see," Tommy said, "appears to be a normal business structure. No scams at any point, that at least Kenyon knows about."

"From what I can tell from him," Jewel said, "Kenyon would be mortified if he had a scam like the one in Portland anywhere along his command."

"I agree," Gail said.

Sunset had to agree as well. Everything he was seeing through Kenyon made this all appear to be a very legitimate business.

"So why was this guy brainwashed with a Mind Stone?" Jewel asked. "I'm going to go exploring back in his memories before the brainwashing."

When she came back a moment later she said, "Let's get out of this guy's head and talk."

All four of them stepped back into the plush office as Kenyon kept working on a merger document he had been reading between a firm in Sweden and one based in Germany.

"This guy is no different before the brainwashing than after," Jewel said.

"So why is it there?" Gail asked.

Sunset knew the answer almost instantly. "It's a time bomb."

Jewel nodded. "That's my guess also. But we need to see if Kenyon is the only one who is the same before and after that lump of brainwashing."

They all nodded and headed for different offices.

Twenty minutes later they were standing in the wide hallway near a receptionist desk and a bank of elevators.

"They are all the same before and after," Tommy said.

Sunset agreed. "And I tried to get near one of the lumps of brainwashing. My sense is if triggered, it will expand and just shut down the person."

"I saw the same thing," Jewel said. "Everyone will simply fall over, not dead, but trapped in their own minds as we did with Cadmus."

"Why?" Gail asked.

"These seven major businesses control a vast number of the world's banking and investments and corporations," Tommy said.

"Everyone running them falls over," Sunset said, "it will send the world's economies into the dark ages."

"Not counting the panic of just having that many people suddenly appear sick," Jewel said.

"Oh, we are so screwed," Gail said.

Sunset could only agree to that.

Twenty-Six

Gail sat next to Sunset in the booth in Poker Boy's floating office. Tommy and Jewel sat on chairs at the end of the table, leaving room for Laverne on one side. They were the only four there at the moment.

After realizing what might happen, she and Sunset and Jewel and Tommy had spread out through the two buildings, making sure that nothing was different.

And then they had gone to the other six business headquarters and gone inside the heads of the other six presidents. All were the same as Kenyon.

All had what appeared to be a ticking time bomb in their heads, ready to go off and shut them down instantly.

So after four hours, they all decided it was time to tell Poker Boy and Laverne what they had found, see if any of them had any ideas.

Gail was flat scared for what would happen if something

triggered all those planted bombs, as they were calling them. They had no idea how all of them would be triggered. From what they could tell, it had taken years and years to plant them all.

But there must have been a reason.

Madge brought the four of them burgers and fries and shakes, which looked amazing and smelled even better. As they were digging into the food, Poker Boy arrived with Ben and sat across from her and Sunset.

Poker Boy never seemed to take off the leather coat and black fedora-like hat.

"Wow, those smell wonderful," Poker Boy said.

"Help yourself," Sunset said. "We're only eating the ghost elements, remember?"

Sunset pulled the entire cheeseburger ghost plate and burger toward him, leaving the original.

"Oh, yeah," Poker Boy said, smiling, taking the original and pulling it closer.

Ben just took a few fries and sat back, saying nothing.

At that moment Laverne appeared and sat down, taking one of Gail's fries.

"So how bad is it?" she asked, looking sideways at Jewel and Tommy.

"Bad," Tommy said.

"Really bad," Jewel said.

Gail found herself nodding to that.

Jewel told Laverne what each person that they had seen had in their heads.

"Time bombs?" Poker Boy asked.

"That's what we are calling it," Gail said.

"It will do to each person who has it inside," Sunset said, "when triggered, basically what we did to Cadmus."

Laverne just shook her head and Poker Boy sat there not showing any emotion at all.

"So how did these all get implanted?" Laverne asked.

"A computer program of some sort," Jewel said. "From what we can tell. But it is not altering in any way the person's thoughts or activities. It is just sitting there dormant."

"So a lot of people not working for those companies might have it as well," Poker Boy said.

The four Ghost Agents just nodded. That was something they had figured out fairly quickly that this might have spread far, far beyond the businesses.

"We think," Jewel said, turning slightly in her chair so that she could face Laverne, "that there are more Mind Stones out there."

Laverne slowly nodded. "I have been afraid of that for more centuries than I want to count."

"We believe that Cadmus had two partners in all this," Jewel said, going on. "Two men by the name of Rhesus and Sinon."

Laverne blinked.

From what Gail could tell, Lady Luck was actually surprised.

"Ben," Laverne said. "Do you know those two names?"

Ben nodded. "Lower level workers on Olympus. They have been a couple since before Atlantis. They were support in the fight against the Titans."

Laverne turned back to Jewel. "You are sure those are the names?"

Jewel nodded.

Gail found herself nodding as well.

"The three of them were the brains and money behind the entire seven massive businesses," Tommy said. "From what we can tell, they have been building these businesses for most of the last century and through this century."

"They were in the fight with the Titans," Ben said. "As was everyone from Olympus. So they might have obtained Mind Stones. But I doubt they would have had the power to use them."

"Cadmus might have trained them," Poker Boy said. "Is that possible?"

Laverne nodded slowly.

"Would it take a Mind Stone to trigger the shut-down reaction?" Poker Boy asked.

Ben shrugged.

"I honestly don't know," Laverne said. "But I will find out."

Gail wasn't happy with the sound of that.

Laverne looked at Jewel and Tommy. "Would it be possible for me to get inside Cadmus's head, talk with him, without you releasing him?"

It took a moment, but slowly Gail and Tommy both nodded.

"We could take you in," Jewel said.

"Then we need to do that now," Laverne said, standing. She looked at Ben. "Tell Gail and Sunset and Poker Boy about those two others, find their location, and scout them out. We need to know if they have Mind Stones as well. And if they really are connected with all this."

Jewel and Tommy stood and a moment later the three of them were gone.

Heavy silence filled the floating office and the large booth.

Gail did not envy Jewel and Tommy having Laverne ride along with them into the head of another very angry god.

Gail had only been a Ghost Agent for a very short time and already so much of this was so far over her head. Doing something like that would scare her silly.

She would do it if she had to. But she was really glad she didn't have to.

Twenty-Seven

Sunset went back to working on his burger and fries and milkshake while Poker Boy jumped Ben to his office to get information on Rhesus and Sinon. There had been a number of things in that conversation that Sunset had desperately wanted to ask about. But the time wasn't right, clearly.

Gail leaned against him for a moment, then also went back to eating. With the way things were going, there was no telling when they would be able to eat again, so they might as well do it now while they had a break.

Sunset hadn't gotten more than a few bites into his burger when Poker Boy and Ben returned.

"I was remembering them right," Ben said as they slid into the booth and Poker Boy went back to eating as well. "Rhesus and Sinon are low-level gods who have been here since the beginning. They have made no trouble at all and just stayed together and to themselves, only coming forward to help when asked."

"So this sort of plan to drop the world back into the dark ages isn't their style?" Poker Boy asked.

"Sure doesn't seem like it would be," Sunset said.

"I agree," Ben said. "But over centuries people do change."

Sunset just shook his head at that. He had been a ghost for over a hundred years. He still couldn't imagine centuries.

Beside him Gail was staring at her fries and just shaking her head, clearly having the same trouble.

"So do you think they will remember you?" Poker Boy asked Ben.

"I would imagine they would, yes," Ben said.

"So why don't we all four just go talk with them," Poker Boy said. "Ben, you and I from the outside, Gail and Sunset from the inside."

"Seems like as good an idea as any," Ben said.

Sunset and Gail and Poker Boy all took one last bite of their burgers while Ben took another fry.

Then they jumped into the warm Las Vegas air.

In front of them was a walled compound with a wide driveway leading through a high metal gate. The grounds were beautiful, from what Sunset could see through the gate, decorated in that desert rock and sand, with low-water plants everywhere and a number of large trees up closer to the main house inside the walls.

Poker Boy went over and hit the call button on the wall. A moment later a voice came back with simply "Yes."

"Ben and Poker Boy here to see Rhesus and Sinon."

There was silence for a moment, then the gate clicked. "Please, come in."

The four of them walked up the wide driveway toward the large brown stucco home covering a small hilltop. It was a massive mansion, but there were bigger in Las Vegas. And even though this showed money, it didn't shout it as Cadmus's compound had.

A man in silk slacks and a pink golf shirt and no shoes met them at the massive front door to the mansion. His hair was colored blonde and swept back off his forehead. He had to have two rings, at least, on each finger. Not cheap rings, either.

He was smiling showing perfect teeth and clearly surprised and happy to see Ben and Poker Boy.

"Rhesus," Ben said, "I'd like you to meet Poker Boy."

Poker Boy nodded, bowing slightly. "Pleasure is all mine."

"Oh, heavens, no, it is our honor," Rhesus said, almost giggling. "Come in. Come in. Sinon is so flustered he had to run and change clothes. I told him he looked fine but he would have none of it."

Sunset and Gail stood off to one side, saying nothing, as Rhesus let Poker Boy and Ben into the vast mansion.

Then Sunset and Gail followed.

The ceilings of the place were so high and the entrance so large, with large stone columns and stone floors, the place almost echoed like a canyon.

Sunset took Gail's hand and they stepped into Rhesus.

Sunset was shocked. He wasn't sure what he was expecting, but Rhesus was on the inside exactly how he presented on the outside. He and Sinon had been a couple for more centuries than Sunset wanted to look at.

And they didn't care at all about money. They made enough to live in their style of comfort and that was it.

And there was a time bomb in him as well.

"This guy isn't smart enough to do this sort of major plot," Gail said after a moment.

"We saw that Kenyon and the other six corporation heads were reporting to them," Sunset said. "But I see no evidence at all that is the case."

"And I see no sign at all," Gail said, "that they know what a Mind Stone is."

"They are being used," Sunset said. "Just as Cadmus was being used."

Rhesus had shown Poker Boy and Sunset into a massive library with large couches and chairs and a massive stone fireplace. The shelves were all dark maple and every shelf seemed to be jammed with ancient books.

"It is so unusual that we get guests," Rhesus said.

"We need to go all the way back in this guy's mind to see if we are missing something," Sunset said.

"I agree," Gail said. "Look for any sign of the Mind Stones being with them."

Like pealing an onion, Sunset drifted back into the depths of Rhesus's memories, back before Atlantis, back to the fight with the Titans to save Earth.

Turns out the Titans were aliens. And the gods were not yet gods, but more of a major ship's crew.

"Here," Gail said.

Sunset went to her.

It was in a memory, right after the Titans had been defeated, that Rhesus picked up two Mind Stones. He did not know what they were, but thought them attractive. So he kept them.

The necklaces, along with all the other jewelry of Rhesus and Sinon, moved with them for centuries, finally ending up, as far as Rhesus knew, in their vault under the house. He had no idea what they were and had not given them a thought.

"Got a hunch they are not in the vault," Gail said.

"Got a hunch you are right," Sunset said. "Shall we go tell Ben and Poker Boy what we have found?"

They emerged from Rhesus just as Sinon made his entrance. And an entrance he made. Some of the best drag queens in all of Las Vegas would be jealous of Sinon.

His thick makeup was perfect, his long brown hair pulled up and tucked on his head, his jewelry stunning and large. He looked to be about five-foot even, including his heels which he walked in without a problem. He wore thinning silk slacks, a frilly silk blouse, and a scarf of rainbow colors around his neck.

Ben and Poker Boy both stood when he entered and introduced themselves.

As Sinon was working to offer Ben and Poker Boy a snack from a tray of small pastries on a nearby mantle, Sunset told Ben and Poker Boy what they had found.

"We'll check Sinon now," Gail said, "but I am not

expecting anything to be different. They did not know what the Mind Stones were when they found them."

Sunset followed Gail into Sinon and found exactly the same thing as they had found in Rhesus. The two had been together for more centuries than Sunset could imagine and that impressed him.

As the four live humans were finally getting settled on the couches facing each other, Sunset and Gail stepped out of Sinon.

"The same as expected," Sunset said and then he and Gail stepped back.

"To what do we owe this honor?" Rhesus asked.

"Actually," Ben said, "we believe you might help us track down two pendants that are required in a fight we are waging at the moment. We believe you might have found them back right after the war with the Titans."

"A terrible time," Sinon said, fanning himself with an imaginary fan.

"We picked up a lot of trinkets and jewelry after that war," Rhesus said.

Ben went on to describe the two Mind Stones and Rhesus nodded.

"We have two of them," Rhesus said.

"Would it be possible for us to borrow them?" Poker Boy asked.

"If it will help your team and Laverne save the world yet again," Rhesus said, "I am sure we can part with them."

"Oh, heavens yes," Sinon said, standing. "They are in the vault. I will lead the way."

Rhesus smiled fondly as he and Ben and Poker Boy stood and followed Sinon.

They took a hidden elevator down three floors. It was behind what looked like a normal hallway panel of wood with an original Picasso on it.

A large stone chamber was at the bottom of the elevator, lined with shelves and full of furniture and pottery of various types.

A large vault door was against the far wall and Rhesus took only a moment to open it, leading all of them into a massive bank-like vault full of drawers and drawers of jewelry and stones.

All Sunset could do was shake his head. Amazing what collecting could do if a person could manage it for thousands and thousands of years.

"They are here," Rhesus said, pulling open one drawer about halfway down the room.

The drawer was empty, as both Sunset and Gail expected it would be.

Rhesus just stared.

Sinon took one look in the drawer and fainted dead away.

The Mind Stones were gone.

Twenty-Eight

Gail watched as Rhesus tried to help Sinon back to his feet on those heels he wore. Not an easy task.

"We'll see if we can figure out what happened," Gail said to Poker Boy and Ben.

"I'll take Rhesus," Sunset said.

Gail nodded and a moment later was inside Sinon. But instead of looking generally at things, she focused down on any access he might have done with the vault, or with anyone else in the vault.

Gail could tell that the two had been very careful. Not even their employees knew how to get into the vault. And almost no one knew it was even there.

But a god like Cadmus, if they knew where the vault was, could teleport inside and get the stones and take them.

Gail worked her way back through Sinon's mind, ignoring

all the lifestyle things she flat didn't want to know about, and focusing on the vault.

As far as Sinon was concerned, no one had been in that vault since they built it fifty years before. And the stones were there at that point because he had put them there.

As the four live humans returned to the library, Gail left Sinon.

A moment later Sunset appeared from Rhesus.

"I have nothing," Gail said.

"They had not thought of those two stones since they built the vault," Sunset said, "and no one but someone who could teleport could have gotten in there."

Ben and Poker Boy both nodded. "I'm afraid we need to get going. We now must find out who stole your pendants."

"Please do," Rhesus said as he comforted Sinon who had dropped into a chair and looked faint again.

"Thank you for your time," Ben said.

"Yes, thank you," Poker Boy said, bowing to both gods slightly.

Then they vanished.

Sunset and Gail stayed for a moment longer, until Sinon burst into tears and started sobbing about how much of a fool they had made of themselves.

The noise was like a bad actor on a stage thinking he had to project the sobs to the back row.

"You want to help them?" Sunset asked.

Gail shook her head. "This is their relationship. Rhesus will take care of it."

Sunset just shook his head. "Poor man."

"It's worked for them for more centuries than I can imagine," Gail said.

Again Sunset just shook his head as Sinon kept sobbing, getting snot all over his perfect outfit.

Gail took Sunset by the hand and a moment later they were in Poker Boy's office and away from the sobbing god.

And the silence was wonderful.

Twenty-Nine

S unset and Gail slid back into the giant diner booth across from Poker Boy and Ben. Sunset just stared through the windows of the floating office and out over Las Vegas. The sky was a deep blue and the distant mountains looked closer because the air was so clear.

A couple of airliners were circling for approach into McCarran and a small plane was climbing away toward Lake Mead in the distance.

A beautiful day, and one he and Gail would have enjoyed if the world didn't feel like it was about to end.

Madge hadn't taken away the basket of fries, so both he and Gail started munching on them. They were almost as good cold as warm.

Poker Boy and Ben just sat silently, clearly lost in their own thoughts.

Finally Poker Boy said, "Not a bit of this makes sense."

With that, Sunset agreed. Nothing at all about any of this made sense.

"So correct me if I am wrong," Poker Boy said. "We have seven major businesses, as far as we can tell, completely legit. Right?"

Sunset nodded. "Yes, and we have checked them all. They are all aboveboard and report to two people called Rhesus and Sinon, but clearly not the originals."

"And there are two more Mind Stones, right?" Poker Boy asked. "Stolen from that vault."

Gail and Sunset both nodded to that.

"And the only way to take anything from that vault would be to teleport in there and get them," Poker Boy said. "And yet no one really knew they were there. Just makes no sense."

"And what is making even less sense to me," Sunset said, "is where did the vast amounts of money come from to start up these two major conglomerates?"

"And for what reason?" Gail said.

"Not a bit of sense at all," Poker Boy said again, shaking his head and going back to staring off into space.

Sunset munched on a fry and did the same thing.

"The key," Ben said, speaking up for the first time, "is who knew Rhesis and Sinon had those stones."

Poker Boy nodded. And knew them well enough that they could safely be used as patsies."

At that moment Laverne and Jewel and Tommy appeared and sat down in the chairs facing the large table.

Sunset was shocked at how shaken all three seemed.

"Cadmus knew about the other two Mind Stones,"

Laverne said, her voice cold and angry. "He was the one who jumped into their vault and stole them."

"That answers that one question," Poker Boy said.

Sunset just nodded.

"He does not know where they are now," Jewel said. "He lost control of them forty years ago."

"This has been building for that long?" Poker Boy asked, sounding as shocked as Sunset felt.

"Yes," Laverne said.

"Wow, talk about a long game," Poker Boy said, sitting back.

Sunset looked at Laverne, who also seemed to be lost in thought. But he needed to know the big answer.

"Do you know who Cadmus gave the Mind Stones to?"

Laverne nodded, along with Jewel and Tommy.

"He gave them to Alecto and Demeter."

"Oh, no," Ben said softly.

"Two of the Furies?" Gail asked, clearly shocked.

Laverne nodded.

Sunset had no idea who they were, but from Ben's reaction and Gail's question, it didn't sound good.

"So why the time bombs in people's heads?" Sunset asked.

"Revenge," Laverne said simply. "I imprisoned them for a few thousand years. They plan on getting back at me by destroying the world I help defend."

"Oh," was all Sunset could think of to say.

Thirty

Gail watched as Laverne vanished, saying she was going to check on any progress Dottie and Harmony were making.

"Someone want to fill me in on the history of Alecto and Demeter?" Poker Boy asked.

Gail knew the Greek history of the two, but from what she had been learning just the last day or so, the history often shadowed but was not exactly accurate when it came to gods.

"There were three of them originally, sisters called The Furies," Ben said. "One was killed in the battle with the Titans and that turned the other two angry, to say the least. They blamed their sister's death on Zeus and Laverne for even getting them into the war."

"So how did they end up in prison?" Sunset asked a moment before Gail could.

"When Atlantis fell," Ben said, "they profited from the

pain and death and set up massive estates in central Germany. Laverne jailed them. They were released by the Fates about five hundred years ago and vanished."

Gail glanced at Jewel and Tommy, who were being very quiet after their experience in Cadmus's mind.

"Does Cadmus know where they are located?" Gail asked.

Both Jewel and Tommy shook their heads.

"And he does not know about the time bombs they planted either," Tommy said. "He thought it was all about making money and getting control of a vast part of the world's businesses."

"So how do we first find them and then stop them?" Poker Boy asked.

Silence met that question around the floating office.

Finally Ben said simply, "If we find them, we get the Mind Stones. Without the Mind Stones, they should not be able to trigger the time bombs in people's heads."

"So we go after the Mind Stones," Poker Boy said.

Gail liked how Poker Boy always seemed to be in charge without ever really acting like he was in charge. A trait of a true leader.

Then Gail heard herself think the word charge and had a thought. "Ben, since we have one Mind Stone, would the stones be linked in some sort of power connection in any way?"

"Something we could trace?" Sunset asked, following exactly what she was thinking.

Ben sat for a moment. Silence filled the office.

Then he said, "It's an alien technology, so I don't know for certain. But it might be possible. Laverne?"

Laverne appeared standing at the end of the table. Ben quickly told her Gail's question.

Laverne nodded after a moment. "It might be possible. What would you need to figure that out?"

"I'll need to run some tests on Olympus," Ben said.

Laverne nodded. "Do it. Stan, please jump with Ben to Olympus."

Stan, the God of Poker, appeared a moment later and then he and Ben vanished.

"I will tell Dottie and Harmony what they are doing," Laverne said, and vanished.

That left the four ghosts and Poker Boy at the table.

Gail looked at Poker Boy. "Olympus still exists?"

Poker Boy just shook his head. "You wouldn't believe me if I told you."

Gail laughed. "After the last few days, you would be surprised at what I would believe."

Sunset, Jewel, and Tommy all nodded to that as Madge appeared from behind the booth carrying new batches of hot French fries and cheeseburgers.

And the wonderful smell changed the topic perfectly.

Thirty-One

After fifteen more minutes of talking, they had come up with nothing more, so Poker Boy said he was going to go try to explain to Patty what had happened.

Jewel and Tommy jumped home to rest and Sunset jumped Gail and himself back to their condo in Portland.

The day there was as beautiful as it was in Las Vegas. Only greener.

The rivers were glistening in the sunlight and the view just stopped him cold. Amazing how being threatened with the end of civilization made him appreciate it even more.

They both climbed into the shower and then into bed, mostly without talking. They both needed a nap and the next thing Sunset realized, Gail was bringing him a cup of coffee that smelled wonderful.

She had gotten up and dressed and gone down to the

Starbucks on the corner to get coffee and some pastries for both of them.

They sat in her dining area, staring out at the view. The sun was already low enough now in the west to put much of the downtown Portland area in shadows. But Mt. Hood, with the early winter snow, was bright white in the sunlight.

The coffee and pastry helped and as he was about to finish the last bite, Gail said, "Another thing makes no sense."

"Add it to the list in this craziness," Sunset said, laughing. "So what is our new addition?"

"Why use a Mind Stone for basically a small job like was done in this investment company here? It doesn't fit the pattern we are uncovering at all."

Sunset sat back, feeling slightly stunned. She was right. It didn't fit the pattern, yet when Harmony and Dottie tried to trace it, they had been trapped by Cadmus in a memory of Atlantis.

"Harmony and Dottie knew what had been used was a Mind Stone," Sunset said, forcing himself to think this through. "And they figured they needed the thing that Harmony had to block the powers. Right?"

"They called it the Necklace Stone," Gail said, nodding.

"So maybe this Necklace can stop this, if there are more of them," Sunset said. "But we just have no idea what it does."

"It seemed very important and then all of us sort of forgot it," Gail said. "Seems like we need to remind people of it."

"It does seem that way."

Gail called Jewel and Tommy and a moment later they appeared. They both looked refreshed as well.

It only took a minute to explain to them what they were wondering about the Necklace Stone.

"Laverne," Jewel said looking slightly upward at the ceiling on the condo. "We have an idea, but need a few answers first."

Laverne's voice came back strong. "Poker Boy's office."

The four of them jumped there instantly.

From a fantastic view overlooking the green and water of Portland, Oregon, to an even more fantastic view overlooking the brown desert and mountains around Las Vegas, it was just late enough in the day that the lights of the Strip were starting to take over from the daylight.

Poker Boy and Ben were sitting in the booth when they arrived and a moment later Laverne appeared. Clearly Ben had managed to finish his research.

After they were all seated, Sunset decided he was going to get right to the point. He looked at Laverne and said simply, "Why was the Necklace Stone so important when we first started this? What does it do?"

"And how many of them are there?" Gail asked.

Laverne actually frowned.

Poker Boy shook his head and muttered, "Forgot all about that."

"The Necklace Stone is a name for an ancient alien device that blocks the powers of the Mind Stones," Ben said. "Which are also alien devices. There was only one Necklace Stone known to exist."

"But until today there was only one Mind Stone known to exist, correct?" Poker Boy asked.

Laverne nodded.

"So why do the scam in Portland?" Sunset asked, deciding to continue directly at the topic that bothered him. "What purpose did that do?"

"It brought the Necklace Stone out of hiding," Poker Boy said.

"Shit!" Laverne said and vanished.

Silence filled the office.

Deadly silence.

When Lady Luck herself swears, you know something is very, very wrong.

A few long moments later she appeared with Dottie and Harmony, both looking a little shocked.

"Is the Necklace Stone still on you?" Laverne asked Harmony.

She nodded and showed Laverne, who looked visibly relieved.

She indicated that the two ancient gods should join them at the table and Sunset and Gail scooted clear around to the back of the booth to let Jewel and Tommy into the booth.

Sunset was having trouble coming to terms that he was not only dealing with Poker Boy, but there were four ancient gods sitting in this old diner booth with him.

Laverne tuned to Ben. "What did your research on Olympus discover about the Mind Stones?"

"Nothing new, I'm afraid," Ben said. "The Necklace Stone can block the effect."

"Can we produce more Necklaces?" Sunset asked, speaking before he realized even what he was thinking.

Silence filled the office again as Ben looked at Sunset, then slowly nodded. "I think we can. Yes."

"So what kind of area will the Necklace protect?" Poker Boy asked.

"I honestly don't know," Ben said. "But I did discover that the Necklace Stone gives off a very specific signal. From Olympus, I should be able to track if there are more of them."

Sunset understood devices far, far better than he understood what some of the gods could do, so it was a relief to him that they were talking about the Necklace Stone as nothing more than a screening device.

"If that signal the Necklace Stone is emitting could be expanded," Sunset said, "or enough Necklace Stones produced, to cover the globe with their blocking signal, we would not have to ever worry about the time bombs in people's minds being triggered by the Mind Stones."

Laverne nodded. "Ben, do you and a few others need Harmony's Necklace Stone to do the research to find out if what Sunset suggested is possible?"

"No," Ben said. "But I do have a way that using Harmony's Necklace Stone, you might be able to trace other Necklace Stones. But I think it is something only our Ghost Agent friends here will be able to see."

Ben smiled at the shocked look on Sunset's face.

"Harmony, would you take your Necklace and hold it out?" Ben asked.

Harmony did, holding out the flat long crystal stone in her hand and leaving the cord around her neck.

"Now," Ben said. "My understanding is that Ghost Agents can see auras, correct?"

"Yes, but we keep it dampened most of the time," Jewel said. "Too distracting."

Sunset agreed with that. If he didn't dampen his vision of people's auras, he would have gone crazy a century before.

"Turn it back on now," Ben said.

Sunset did as Ben suggested, at first blinded by the huge and intense and powerfully bright aura of Laverne.

All four Ghost Agents shielded their eyes.

"Laverne," Jewel said. "Could you and Dottie please move around behind the booth for a moment."

Dottie and Laverne did, leaving only the very bright aura of Harmony, shimmering in bright gold and green colors.

Stunningly beautiful.

But then Sunset looked at the Harmony stone and he could see the web of energy coming off of it, expanding like a web over the entire office.

"It is clear," Jewel said. "Like a net over all of us."

"See if you can see a string of the energy leaving the localized net," Ben said.

Jewel and Tommy both stood and then both of them floated up and out through the office walls, just seeming to stand out in the air, studying everything.

Silence once again as Sunset watched. He didn't know that Ghost Agents could float like that. Clearly something he and Gail needed to learn.

After a full minute of everyone watching them through the windows, they came back inside.

"There are hundreds of lines of power leaving this net in all directions," Jewel said.

"Maybe upward of three hundred by my quick count," Tommy said.

"You think they all lead to other Necklace Stones?" Laverne asked.

Ben nodded. "I do. I think every Necklace Stone is connected to every other Necklace Stone."

"Oh, wow, we might not need to produce more," Jewel said.

Sunset could only hope she was right.

Thirty-Two

Gail was stunned when Jewel and Tommy just sort of floated out into the air a thousand feet above Las Vegas Boulevard. That must have been something to feel.

Clearly floating like that was something that hadn't been in her training. But she wanted it to be and soon. She had always dreamed of flying and she had a hunch that is exactly what that would feel like.

When Jewel and Tommy came back and reported a possible hundreds more Necklace Stones, she actually felt excited.

Laverne nodded to the news. She turned to Ben. "Get Stan and head back to Olympus and figure out how to expand the protection of the Necklace Stones.

Ben nodded and a moment later Stan appeared and then the two of them vanished.

Laverne turned to Dottie and Harmony. "I would like you two to keep working on the computer side of things. We still need to know where Alecto and Demeter are. And protect that Necklace Stone. But don't go just yet. I need the Ghost Agents to follow the trail from your Necklace Stone to others first."

Both nodded.

Then Laverne turned to Poker Boy. "Put all of your team on alert. You are going to be getting the Necklace Stones when the Ghost Agents locate them. We might need them at a moment's notice."

He nodded. "Back in five minutes." Then he vanished.

Laverne turned to Gail and the other three Ghost Agents. "I need you four to spread out and follow those energy lines to other Necklace Stones. Then tell Poker Boy to bring them back here. I will collect them and keep them safe until Ben figures out how to use them."

The four Ghost Agents nodded.

They all stood as Madge brought burgers and fries and vanilla milkshakes for Laverne, Dottie, and Harmony.

"Gail and I have a problem," Sunset said to Jewel and Tommy as they moved toward the edge of the office. "We don't know how to fly like that yet."

Gail was very happy Sunset had told them instead of her.

Jewel and Tommy both smiled and nodded.

"There is no trick to it," Tommy said. "You know how you were able to jump to a new place by just imagine being there?"

Gail nodded.

"Just imagine yourself lifting off the ground, being lighter than air," Jewel said. "Same thing."

"Remember we are ghosts," Tommy said. "We don't really exist in any form other than what we imagine. We can transport, walk through things, so we can float as well."

Gail nodded and just focused and imagined herself lifting into the air from the floor.

Next thing she knew she was going through the glass ceiling of Poker Boy's office and out into the warm air of the desert. There was a pretty good wind, but it didn't seem to affect her at all, even though she could feel it.

It felt so wonderful to just float in the sky, she just wanted to shout for joy. She had no fear at all.

Sunset floated up right beside her, a smile on his face so wide he looked like a kid. She imagined she was smiling just as much.

Tommy and Jewel joined them, also both smiling.

"Fun, isn't it?" Tommy asked.

All Gail could do was nod, enjoying the feeling of floating like a kid's balloon.

As all four of them floated there, Jewel pointed back at the office below them. "See the web of bright white lines around everything?"

Gail looked and nodded. It was as if the floating office had a bright fisherman's net around it.

And moving away from the net were hundreds of lines going in all directions.

Five actually went down to different spots in the Las Vegas area.

"Let's all four follow that one," Tommy said, pointing to one that dropped toward the downtown area. "See what is at the other end."

As one they flew along the white energy line. Gail had no doubt that they could go faster, but even going slowly, they reached the other end of the line within a few seconds.

The Necklace Stone was being used as decoration in a landscaping area near a sidewalk in the Golden Nugget Pool area. It had a large net radiating out around it as well.

And hundreds and hundreds of power lines radiating off from it as well.

"Poker Boy," Jewel said into the air as the four of them stood around the Necklace Stone. "Can you jump to me?"

A moment later Poker Boy appeared in the pool area and Gail noticed that he had formed a pocket of time around himself and them, making everyone in the pool area seem to freeze. She had heard he could do that, seemingly stop time. It was creepy because all sound suddenly stopped.

And all the people around the pool were frozen in bizarre postures.

She knew Poker Boy had to do that to make sure the cameras and all the people around in the pool area didn't just see him appear.

Jewel bent down and pointed at the stone that was almost too bright to look at.

Poker Boy picked it up and studied it. Gail turned off her aura vision so she could actually see it as well. It was long and shaped like a crystal and sort of a gray color.

"They sure don't look like much, do they?" he said.

Gail had to agree, they didn't.

He nodded and vanished, letting time crash back in around the four Ghost Agents.

The sounds of the living hit hard. Amazing how you don't notice sounds until there was a complete lack of sound.

Gail turned back on her aura vision and all the white lines that had come off the Necklace Stone were gone.

"Back to Poker Boy's office to plan this," Jewel said.

When they appeared in Poker Boy's office, the net around the place had doubled and the lines leading off to other stones were now much brighter.

Gail could only imagine what this place would look like when they had hundreds of those stones here.

She just hoped that nothing would go wrong with that many stones that close together.

Thirty-Three

Three hours later, Sunset found his sixtieth stone on a rocky beach just along the English coast. The weather there was cold and the wind biting.

He quickly called for Poker Boy, who appeared, took the stone Sunset was pointing to and vanished, all within ten seconds.

Sunset jumped back to floating above Poker Boy's office just as Gail appeared.

"Traced another one under water," she said. "That's six for me under water."

"Eight," Sunset said.

They had been discovering that many of the stones were in lakes or deep in oceans. They could go in and down into depths, but none of the gods could follow them to actually pick up the stones. So they were going to wait until Sunset figured out what was possible before trying to retrieve those.

Both Tommy and Jewel were convinced that if they needed to, they could pick up the stones and get them to the surface.

Sunset was convinced he couldn't. He could barely move a plate on a table, let along pick up something and try to bring it up through water.

A moment later Jewel appeared and then a moment after that, Tommy. All four of them floated about two hundred feet above Poker Boy's office.

There were so many Necklace Stones in Poker Boy's office, with their aura vision turned on there was a glow around the office that glowed almost as bright as a sun.

"I think we have every one not under water," Tommy said.

Gail nodded.

"I bet Poker Boy is exhausted," Sunset said, smiling.

"Let's go find out," Jewel said.

They jumped back inside the office. Sunset made sure his aura vision was off because he flat didn't want to see what it looked like in there with that many Necklace Stones.

"We're sure the rest are all under water," Jewel said to Laverne as the four Ghost Agents scooted into the booth. Dottie and Harmony were gone. A large wicker basket full of Necklace Stones sat beside Laverne. All of them looked exactly the same dull gray.

Poker Boy was sitting in the booth drinking a milkshake and working on a hamburger.

A moment later Madge appeared with burgers and fries and milkshakes for the four of them as well. The food smelled fantastic and he didn't realize how hungry he had become.

At that moment Ben and Stan appeared and joined Poker Boy on the other side of the booth.

Ben saw the basket of stones and nodded.

"Any luck?" Laverne asked.

Ben nodded. "As far as I can tell, there are only three Mind Stones and I think I have a way to trace them now from their energy signal."

"Fantastic," Laverne said, nodding.

"Were you able to get all of the Necklace Stones?" Ben asked.

"No," Laverne said. "About thirty are in oceans and lakes. By my count we have two-hundred and sixty-three in this basket, plus the one Harmony is wearing."

Ben nodded. "That will be enough. We need two-hundred and sixty."

"To do what exactly?" Laverne asked.

"We will need to put the stones we have in exact places along all the major energy lay lines around the planet," Ben said. "I have the exact locations each would need to be placed. Then from Olympus, I should be able to power them up using the lay lines to expand the Necklace Stones' protective area."

"Will it be enough?" Laverne asked.

Ben nodded. "It will form a shield around the planet that will basically make the Mind Stones worthless. But I would not suggest we go after the Mind Stones until we have that in place."

Laverne nodded.

Laverne turned to the Ghost Agents. "Go get some rest.

We're going to need you as soon as we have the shield in place."

Sunset found himself nodding along with Gail and Tommy and Jewel.

Then Laverne turned to Poker Boy. "Get every one of your team who can teleport and have them meet here in ten minutes. I will call Harmony and Dottie to help. We will take the stones to their locations one at a time."

With that Poker Boy and Stan both vanished.

Sunset reached over and took Gail's hand and a moment later they were in their condo in Portland.

The nightlights of the city were beautiful.

You up for a movie?" Gail asked after a moment of both of them just standing in their living room staring at the lights.

"I'll jump down to the theater to get us some popcorn," Sunset said.

Thirty seconds later he was back with a large bucket of the best-smelling popcorn as Gail managed to get a streaming movie going with the remote. She was actually getting better at moving real-world things than he was. And that came in real handy at times.

PART SIX

Pure Evil Does Exist

Thirty-Four

Gail woke first. She and Sunset had both fallen asleep watching a comedy about old guys robbing a bank. Now the screen was just showing other possible movies for them to watch.

The half-eaten bucket of theater popcorn was still on the coffee table, so they hadn't been asleep that long or it would have vanished. It was still dark outside the windows, with the lights of Portland shining bright.

She untangled herself slowly from Sunset and stood, stretching. The clock on the wall in the kitchen said it was just after two in the morning. They had been back in the apartment for six hours.

She had a hunch that was going to be enough time for Poker Boy and his team to set the stones. So they were going to be needed shortly.

She gently woke up Sunset and he sat up straight and yawned as she punched a few buttons on the remote to turn off the television.

They both splashed water on their faces and changed shirts, then jumped to an all-night restaurant just outside of downtown that served a good bar-rush crowd, so there would be lots of choices for them to pick from.

The place smelled wonderful of fresh coffee and bacon. She was surprised at how hungry she was.

She ended up with three eggs, toast, and bacon while he got a plate of pancakes and ham. They found a booth in an area that looked closed and settled in, drinking coffee and eating breakfast.

They had just finished when Jewel and Tommy appeared and slid into the booth with them.

"Laverne says it will be another hour before the protective net goes live," Jewel said. "We wanted to make sure you two were up and ready."

"Ready as we can be considering we have no idea what we are getting into," Gail said.

"Food's good here," Sunset said, pointing at his empty plate.

"Already ate," Tommy said, "but that coffee smells wonderful."

He stood and headed to get him and Jewel a couple cups of coffee.

Gail waited for Tommy to get back, then asked, "You both were in Cadmus's head. He knows Alecto and Demeter. Any idea what we are getting into?"

Jewel glanced at Tommy, then sighed. "Total evil," she said.

"Powerful evil," Tommy said. "I doubt we are going to be able to get to them like we did Cadmus. At least not easily."

"Cadmus was afraid of both of them," Jewel said. "Terrified."

Tommy nodded.

"I'm amazed the gods don't have some sort of police system to take care of their own getting out of line," Sunset said.

"We are the police force," Jewel said.

Tommy nodded. "Laverne runs everything, is the most powerful god of them all, but even she has limits. That's why Poker Boy and his team are there with her and why she is also using us now when we can be helpful."

Gail just shook her head. "She really is Lady Luck?"

"She is," Jewel said. "And she is that powerful."

Gail forced herself to not think about that. At least not at the moment.

"Any idea where this Olympus they keep talking about is at?" Sunset asked.

"Not a clue," Jewel said and Tommy nodded.

"It's not on this planet," Laverne said, appearing in front of the table and grabbing a chair and pulling it over.

Gail glanced around. Everyone in the restaurant had frozen in place, so Laverne had taken them into a space between moments in time where no one would see her.

Gail was surprised that Laverne didn't look tired or even

frazzled in the slightest, even though they must have been working through the entire night.

"Are we ready to go?" Jewel asked.

Laverne nodded. "The Necklace Stone net is in place and turned on. No Mind Stone can work now."

"How long will that network hold together and be powered up?"

"Centuries," Laverne said. "Everyone who has had a time bomb planted in their heads will be long dead by the time that network stops protecting them."

"Wonderful," Sunset said.

Gail nodded to that, feeling a massive sense of relief.

"So have you found Alecto and Demeter?" Tommy asked.

"No," Laverne said. "We will need you four for that to trace the Mind Stone power lines. Once we find them, we will figure out what we can do."

Gail felt her stomach twist.

"Where do we start?" Jewel asked.

"Let's go to Poker Boy's office," Laverne said. "I have a suspicion those two are not far away."

A moment later they were back in Poker Boy's office.

The lights of Las Vegas were bright below them and the mountains dark around the valley. The night sky was clear and a lot of stars could be seen through the glass ceiling.

Poker Boy and Patty, his girlfriend and superhero, sat against each other in the booth, both looking exhausted. There was no one else there.

Gail took Sunset's hand and the four of them stood, waiting for instructions from Lady Luck.

But she hadn't jumped back here with them. She must have had another stop along the way.

So they stood there, the four of them, staring out at the view, waiting.

Thirty-Five

Sunset just waited with Gail, holding her hand, feeling comfort in having her beside him. He couldn't imagine doing any of this stuff without her, even though he had been alone for almost a hundred years. Now, in a very few months, being alone seemed like an impossible, alien thing.

Laverne took almost two minutes to appear. With her were Dottie and Harmony, both clearly sleepy. Laverne must have woken them up.

Dottie carried her computer to the booth table and immediately sat down and opened it up.

Harmony stood beside her, hand on her shoulder.

Laverne watched them get ready as both Poker Boy and Patty perked up, working to wake up as well.

"Ben and Stan are on Olympus, monitoring the safety

net," Laverne said. "If we need a certain type of help, they will be able to give it from there."

Poker Boy and Patty and both older gods nodded.

Sunset had no idea exactly what Laverne was talking about, but it sounded positive at least.

Laverne then turned to the four Ghost Agents. She took the Mind Stone they had taken from Cadmus out of her pocket and held it in her hand.

"This should have an energy radiating from it as the Necklace Stones did," she said. "We believe the Mind Stones will be linked as well."

"We are not going to be able to see the lines of energy with you holding it," Jewel said. "Your aura is far too bright."

Laverne nodded and set the Mind Stone on a chair, then stepped away.

Sunset moved over between the stone and Laverne and turned on his aura sight.

Laverne was right, it had a red tone around it and two red lines left the stone and went out through the window at a downward angle.

"Red power lines," Jewel said. "Two of them aiming downward toward the north. The lines are basically together."

"I suspected they would be here," Laverne said, nodding. "Gail, Sunset, would you two follow the lines. Do not engage, just come back and tell us exactly what you find."

Jewel was about to object, but Laverne held up her hand.

"We'll be right back," Sunset said, taking Gail's hand.

He understood completely what Laverne was thinking.

He and Gail were the least experienced and the most expendable if they ran into trouble. She would need Jewel and Tommy's help to get him and Gail out of trouble if they found it and got stuck somehow.

He and Gail floated out into the cool night air and down along the red line. It was much fainter than the white lines now blanketing everything and a couple of times the red lines seemed to stop at a white Necklace Stone line.

It took them almost a full minute before they found where the red lines ended.

They carefully eased down into what looked like a massive gated mansion on a rock bluff to the north of the city. Guards patrolled the grounds and the paved road coming in was patrolled as well.

They slowly floated down along the red line, hand in hand, drifting first down through the roof and then through an attic until they were floating near a high ceiling in a massive bedroom.

The room was faintly lit and decorated in expensive southwestern style furniture.

Two women were sleeping together in a huge bed. The two red lines ended on each woman's chest.

Sunset squeezed Gail's hand and a moment later they were back in Poker Boy's office.

Sunset let out the breath he was holding for some reason and beside him Gail did the same.

"They are in an estate to the north of town, well guarded," Gail said.

"The two stones are being worn by two women who are sleeping at the moment," Sunset said.

"Those stones will protect them from you entering their minds," Laverne said, shaking her head.

Sunset looked at the stone still sitting on the chair, then back at Laverne as she frowned, trying to figure out something to do.

"You said you could get help from Olympus," Sunset said. "Would it be possible to send a burst of energy along those power lines to heat up those stones, force them to take them off?"

Laverne looked at Sunset for a moment, picked up the Mind Stone from the chair, then nodded and vanished.

"Might as well grab a seat," Poker Boy said. "She might be a while."

All four of them sat down in the booth facing the tired faces of Patty and Poker Boy as Madge appeared with a carafe of coffee and six cups.

"I thought all you served was milkshakes," Poker Boy said, smiling and nodding his thanks as Madge poured him and Pattie both a cup.

"Not even you wants a milkshake at four in the morning," Madge said.

With that she set the pot full of coffee down in front of the four Ghost Agents and vanished behind the booth.

"She is amazing," Gail said.

Sunset had to agree with that.

Poker Boy just laughed. "You have no idea."

Thirty-Six

Gail sat with Sunset for the hour it took until Laverne returned. Outside the floating office, the sun was just starting to color the distant mountains with a faint pink tint.

When Laverne showed up she said, "You four Ghost Agents get to their bedroom. The power is going to hit those Mind Stones in less than three minutes."

Gail felt her stomach tighten around the coffee. If this didn't get those two gods to take off those stones, they might be alerted that what they were doing had been discovered. Then it would be up to the Necklace Stone shield to work and none of them wanted to really trust that.

Laverne then turned to Poker Boy. "You and Patty be ready to jump the moment you get the call from the Ghost Agents."

"I will be with Harmony and Dottie making sure that any signal is blocked coming out of there."

With that she vanished.

"Good luck," Poker Boy said as Gail and Sunset and Jewel and Tommy jumped into the bedroom of the two sleeping gods.

They stood silently off to one side and the two women didn't seem to know they were being watched. Thankfully.

Both women seemed to be in their late thirties. Both had blonde hair and thin faces.

Gail had heard that sometimes gods could sense a Ghost Agent. Clearly these two did not, at least not enough to wake them up.

The red lines between the two Mind Stones around the women's necks were clear as well as the red lines coming in from the other Mind Stone.

Suddenly that red line coming in through the roof to the two stones seemed to glow an intense red. After a moment it was so bright, Gail had to shut down her aura vision and beside her Sunset at first turned away, then shut down his vision as well.

The two gods on the bed jerked, as if being hit with an intense electrical current.

Their hands grabbed for the Mind Stones on their chests, but the stones seemed to be almost stuck there.

Clearly the stones were getting hot, as the skin around the stones on the women's chests started to turn black.

Gail was shocked. This was not what she had imagined would happen.

Then with one final burst of bright hot light, the energy cut off.

The two gods lay silent, clearly unconscious.

But the stones were still on their chests, so none of them could enter their minds.

"We need help." Jewel said. "They are knocked out and still wearing the Mind Stones."

Poker Boy and Patty instantly appeared and moved to the side of the two gods. They carefully worked to take the stones off the women.

"This looks like it hurt some," Poker Boy said as he peeled the stone off one of the women's chest, taking black skin with it.

Patty was having trouble with the other because it was stuck so hard to the skin.

But the moment Poker Boy had the Mind Stone off of the one woman, Jewel and Tommy went inside her.

Less than three seconds later they reappeared.

"She is dead," they said at the same time.

"Laverne!" Poker Boy said as he moved around to help Patty take the other stone off of the second woman. It made a sound Gail didn't want to ever hear again when they pulled it loose.

Laverne appeared just as Jewel and Tommy went into the second woman.

They reappeared a few seconds later.

"She is dead as well."

Laverne just nodded and said nothing.

Poker Boy handed her the two Mind Stones and what was left of the skin of the two women on the stones vanished.

Laverne put the two stones in her pocket.

"Ghost Agents, check everyone in this house for any kind of information," she said. "And first of all, find their computer area."

Gail nodded with Sunset.

"Poker Boy and Patty, guard these two and make sure nothing changes," Laverne said.

Poker Boy nodded, not looking happy with the task.

"I will get Dottie and Harmony and we will be ready to check out the computers here to make sure nothing is set as an automatic trigger."

With that she was gone.

"Computer room first," Jewel said. "Let's split up and find it. Sunset, you and Gail take the kitchen staff area. We'll take the business area."

The next moment Gail was standing beside Sunset in a large kitchen that smelled of fresh coffee, bacon, and fresh bread.

Five minutes later the four Ghost Agents were standing in the large computer area, making sure the two men and two women sitting at stations were not doing anything that needed to be stopped instantly.

They were not. But they had been brainwashed very much like the ones back in Portland, to believe what they were doing was wonderful.

Gail cleared out the brainwashing on one woman back

two years and told her to go home to her husband and children the job had caused her to neglect.

As the last worker left the room, Laverne and Dottie and Harmony appeared and got down to work.

And Sunset and Gail went back to checking everyone they could see and clearing out some brainwashing where they could.

Three full hours later Laverne called them into the computer room to a smiling Dottie and Harmony. Poker Boy and Patty were standing there, holding hands.

"All clear," Harmony said. "We have set worm programs that will spread around the world and destroy the time bombs in people's heads as they see the program."

"It won't get everyone," Dottie said. "But in just a week or so the threat will be over."

"I have taken care of our two deceased problems," Laverne said. "They have already been sent on a path into the sun."

"So once again the team-up of ghosts and superheroes and gods help save the world," Poker Boy said.

He smiled at the four Ghost Agents. "Kinda fun, huh?"

All Gail could do was shake her head and laugh. She wasn't so certain about the fun part, but is sure did feel good.

Real good.

Thirty-Seven

S unset watched as Gail wound her way back through the wood and brass tables at the Golden Nugget Buffet, carrying a plate of food. She looked radiant, even though tired.

He couldn't believe how much in love with her he was. It now seemed like she had always been a part of his life, and always will be. At least he was going to do his best to be on his best behavior to always have her with him.

She set her plate down, leaned over and kissed him, and then sat down to start to dig in.

He had already started eating.

Jewel and Tommy were still at the buffet filling their plates, dodging around the few live humans in the restaurant.

"How about we sleep until noon," Sunset said, "then just lounge around all day."

"I was kind of thinking we might spend part of the afternoon in bed not sleeping," she said, smiling at him.

"I like that idea a lot," he said, smiling back at her.

She looked directly at him, suddenly serious, and said simply, "Thank you."

He was shocked, but smiled. "We haven't spent the afternoon yet. I might be thanking you."

She laughed. "I am sure you will be. But I wanted to thank you for believing in me, training me, letting me become your first partner after a hundred years of working alone."

Sunset reached toward her and took her hand. "It has been my honor."

"This is sure a long way from that coast highway and the front bumper of that truck," she said.

He could tell she was still having trouble grasping the last day or so. Actually, he was as well. They had both learned and seen so much. It was going to take months to talk it all out, he was sure of that.

Jewel and Tommy sat down across from them and started to eat.

"Did we really just save the world?" Gail asked.

Sunset felt the exact same way, shocked at the very idea.

Tommy smiled as he worked on a piece of ham and Jewel nodded.

"We really did," Jewel said.

"And chances are it won't be the last time," Tommy said.

"Yeah," Jewel said, "This is our second or third time in just a year."

"It's not getting old," Tommy said and they all laughed.

Sunset had heard a few comments about the last time. "Wasn't the last saving of the world around Christmas?"

Jewel nodded and smiled again.

"So tell us what happened," Gail said a moment before Sunset could ask the same question.

"Well," Tommy said, "you know how it was hard to understand that there were gods and superheroes over the last day?"

"Let's not forget the fact that Atlantis existed and Olympus is somewhere out in space," Gail said. "Yeah, pretty tough."

"Pretty crazy day," Sunset said. "To use a wild understatement."

"Well imagine our surprise," Jewel said, "when we discovered Santa Claus was real as well."

"Nope," Gail said, shaking her head. "That's just one step too many."

Sunset felt the same way, but he laughed with Tommy and Jewel. It was too silly to even comprehend.

"You'll meet him at the Christmas party," Tommy said.

Jewel nodded. "He likes us because we saved him."

"So we save the world and get to meet Santa Claus," Gail said. "Now I know for sure that I really am dead."

"And still dreaming," Sunset said, smiling at the woman he loved. For months that had been a standing joke between them.

"Of course I'm dreaming," Gail said. "I'm going back to a beautiful condo in Portland and make love to the most handsome man I have ever met. Santa Claus is just going to be a bonus."

Jewel and Tommy and Sunset all laughed so hard Sunset was sure that even the live people in the early morning breakfast buffet could hear them.

Gail just kept on eating.

In over a hundred years of being dead and trying to help people, he had never felt this good.

This much in love.

And this much alive.

And after a long nap, later that afternoon Gail made him feel even more alive.

She had been right. He did end up thanking her.

GHOST
of a CHANCE

The
POKER CHIP

DEAN WESLEY SMITH

Turn the Page to SAMPLE THE NEXT BOOK...

The Poker Chip

CHAPTER ONE

TWENTY-SEVEN MINUTES before she died, Dr. Jewel Kelly stepped out of the front door of her small office in Buffalo Jump, Montana, and set her medical bag on the sidewalk beside her. She then made sure the office door was locked tight. With a control on her key chain, she triggered the alarm. She doubted anyone around this town would take anything, but better safe than sorry.

She picked up her bag, pulled her ski parka in close around her, and stepped over under the eve of Bernie's General Store. Her little office was like an outbuilding off of Bernie's store. Three rooms and a bathroom.

Enough for her to get the job done, but not by much.

She again set her medical bag down on a dry spot near the building and turned to face the small town and wait for her ride.

She was a tall woman at five-ten, with long brown hair she loved to keep pulled back, and green eyes people said could stare right through you. At twenty-five, she liked more than anything else to run to stay fit. And she loved reading a great romance novel. In med school in Seattle, she had had time to run, but not read.

Now she had more than enough time for both. She usually put in a five-mile run up near the high school every afternoon, staying off the main highway as much as possible.

The run every day at least made her feel alive.

A cold mist of a late April spring day covered the main street of Buffalo Jump, Montana, which was also a major two-lane north-south highway. The air had a bite to it, and she had no doubt that later tonight the mist would turn to snow and the road would freeze over.

She had planned to spend the night in her log cabin a half mile to the south of town, in front of a nice fire, sipping on a glass of white wine and reading the new Nora Roberts novel. Then maybe later, after a nice bath, she would have a date with her best friend, Mr. Buzzy. She had a hunch that in Buffalo Jump, Montana, she was going to wear out good old Buzzy before she found a real man she wanted to date.

To her right and south was Jay's Gas and Minimart, across from that was Carol's Restaurant, a diner that actually had some pretty good food and was pretty clean. Beyond that, the two-lane highway disappeared off into the pine forest, now growing dark as the early evening wore on.

That was the road out of these mountains to Missoula.

To her left and north sat the twenty buildings that made up the main part of Buffalo Jump, including an old hardware store and some basic offices, two bars, and two antique stores to catch the occasional tourist who thought to stop.

She had been in the antique stores, but not the bars. She wasn't much of a drinker except for a nice glass of good wine after dinner.

On the other end of town, she could barely see through the light rain the white tower of the only church, a Presbyterian church, whose basement doubled for a meeting room for the big town events. She hadn't been in there yet either. She had never been much of a church-goer back in Boise where she grew up.

A sprawling red-brick school sat off the main street against a pine-covered hillside and serviced all grades for most of the county, with dozens of lumbering, bright-yellow school busses pouring in and out of town every day. There was even had a high school football team.

Her favorite running route was from her office, up past the school, out a dead-end gravel road for two miles, then back.

Right now she could run up the middle of the main street and no one would even notice. There was no traffic at all and just a few cars parked in front of the bars.

A typical late Thursday afternoon in small town Montana.

Silence closed in around her and she shuddered. Not even a slight wind through the pines around the town broke the oppressive stillness.

She pulled her dark-blue ski parka in around her, making

sure it was zipped, then pulled her ski gloves out of her pocket and put them on. She could never seem to be warm enough here, except when sitting in front of the fire in her cabin.

Under the parka, she had on a nice white blouse and today she had worn jeans for only the second time. It seemed everyone else in town wore jeans, including the mayor, who ran the small grocery store, so she might as well.

Besides, jeans were far more comfortable in the cold weather. Not as drafty as the skirts she wore the first month on the job here. Nothing like a cold Montana wind whipping up a skirt and hitting a cotton-covered crotch to give a girl a real thrill.

And not a fun thrill.

She was the town's only doctor, actually the county's only doctor. And at times like this, she had no idea why she had agreed to the tuition deal to practice medicine here. Sure, she got all her debts forgiven, not a small chunk at all, if she stayed five years, but she wasn't sure if she could handle five years out in the middle of nowhere like this, even though her dream had been to be a GP.

She had only been here for six weeks and mostly been bored out of her mind. She didn't drink and she didn't go to church. That didn't leave a lot left to do except exercise, read and give Mr. Buzzy a workout regularly.

She had delivered one baby in the small building the county called a hospital up beside the school. And she had fixed a few broken bones and one concussion from a bar fight.

For one night, she had even had a woman in the little

four-bed hospital with a gall bladder attack. Jewel had to check in on her every hour to make sure the woman didn't get worse and need to take a Life-Flight out to Missoula.

The woman hadn't gotten worse and the woman's husband the next day had driven her to Missoula, four hours away, for the operation.

Today was Jewel's first call for an injury in Jackson Ridge, another small town about twenty miles away on the highway to the north. The call had come into her cell phone from the county sheriff, and he had told her a deputy would pick her up.

She had told the sheriff she had her car and could drive fine, but the sheriff, a man named Martin, insisted a deputy go along with her.

"Trust me," he had said. "The area this call came from is not a place you go in alone. Especially with that little overseas thing you drive."

Clearly, her red Miata had been noticed, and not in a good way.

"Besides," the sheriff had said, "it's going to be snowing soon and the highway's going to be slick. You don't want to be driving after dark out in these woods until you get to know the roads some."

She had thanked the sheriff and said she would be waiting in front of her office in ten minutes.

"Deputy Ralston will be there as quick as he can," the sheriff had said and hung up.

So now she stood under the eve of the general store, moving from foot to foot, her hands deep in her ski parka pockets, watching the excitement of Buffalo Jump on a late Thursday afternoon.

Except for the misting rain, nothing moved.

Nothing.

Total and complete silence.

What the hell had she been thinking coming here?

Keep Reading *The Poker Chip!*

Go to wmgbooks.com

Hear Directly from Dean

Receive exclusive content, keep up with the latest news, releases and so much more—even the occasional giveaway.

Go to deanwesleysmith.com.

Get the latest news and releases from all of the WMG authors and lines, including Dean Wesley Smith, *Pulphouse Fiction Magazine, Smith's Monthly,* and so much more.

Go to wmgbooks.com.

You can also follow Dean on Bookbub.

We value honest feedback, and would love to hear your opinion in a review, if you're so inclined, on your favorite book retailer's site.

Edited by Dean Wesley Smith

PULPHOUSE FICTION MAGAZINE

Pulphouse Fiction Magazine, edited by Dean Wesley Smith, made its return in 2018, twenty years after its last issue.

Each new issue contains about 70,000 words of short fiction. This reincarnation mixes some of the stories from the old *Pulphouse* days with brand-new fiction.

The magazine has an attitude, as did the first run. No genre limitations, but high-quality writing and strangeness.

Go to www.pulphousemagazine.com.

About the Author

DEAN WESLEY SMITH

Considered one of the most prolific writers working in modern fiction, with more than 30 million books sold, writer Dean Wesley Smith published far more than a hundred novels in forty years, and hundreds of short stories across many genres.

At the moment he produces novels in several major series, including the time travel Thunder Mountain novels set in the Old West, the galaxy-spanning Seeders Universe series, the urban fantasy Ghost of a Chance series, a superhero series starring Poker Boy, and a mystery series featuring the retired detectives of the Cold Poker Gang.

His monthly magazine, *Smith's Monthly*, which consists of only his own fiction, premiered in October 2013 and offers readers more than 70,000 words per issue, including a new and original novel every month.

During his career, Dean also wrote a couple dozen *Star Trek* novels, the only two original *Men in Black* novels, Spider-Man and X-Men novels, plus novels set in gaming and television worlds. Writing with his wife Kristine Kathryn Rusch under the name Kathryn Wesley, he wrote the novel for the

NBC miniseries The Tenth Kingdom and other books for *Hallmark Hall of Fame* movies.

He wrote novels under dozens of pen names in the worlds of comic books and movies, including novelizations of almost a dozen films, from *The Final Fantasy* to *Steel* to *Rundown*.

Dean also worked as a fiction editor off and on, starting at Pulphouse Publishing, then at *VB Tech Journal*, then Pocket Books, and now at WMG Publishing, where he and Kristine Kathryn Rusch serve as series editors for the acclaimed *Fiction River* anthology series.

For more information about Dean's books and ongoing projects, please visit his website at www.deanwesleysmith.com and sign up for his newsletter.

For more information:
www.deanwesleysmith.com

f facebook.com/deanwsmith3
P patreon.com/deanwesleysmith
BB bookbub.com/authors/dean-wesley-smith

Printed in the USA
CPSIA information can be obtained
at www.ICGtesting.com
CBHW021215310824
13887CB00010B/394